fairest
of them
all

fairest
of them
all

Jan Blazanin

Pocket Books   MTV Books
New York London Toronto Sydney

 **BOOKS**

Pocket Books
A Division of Simon & Schuster, Inc.
1230 Avenue of the Americas
New York, NY 10020

First MTV Books/Pocket Books trade paperback edition April 2009

POCKET and colophon are registered trademarks of Simon & Schuster, Inc.

For information about special discounts for bulk purchases,
please contact Simon & Schuster Special Sales at
1-800-456-6798 or business@simonandschuster.com.

Designed by Carla Jayne Little

Manufactured in the United States of America

10 9 8 7 6 5 4 3 2

Library of Congress Cataloging-in-Publication Data

Blazanin, Jan.
  Fairest of them all / Jan Blazanin. — 1st MTV Books/Pocket Books trade pbk. ed.
     p. cm.
  Summary: When gorgeous fifteen-year-old model, dancer, and aspiring actress Oribella Bettancourt develops alopecia and starts losing her trademark long blond hair, it forces both her and her doting mother to reassess their hopes and dreams.
  [1. Beauty, Personal—Fiction. 2. Beauty culture—Fiction. 3. Alopecia areata—Fiction. 4. Baldness—Fiction. 5. Self-perception—Fiction. 6. Mothers and daughters—Fiction.] I. Title.
  PZ7.B61636Fai 2009
  [Fic]—dc22   2008046121

ISBN-13: 978-1-4165-7993-9
ISBN-10:   1-4165-7993-1

For Roberta

Acknowledgments

For my magical writing group, Sharelle Byars Moranville, Eileen Boggess, and Becky Janni, a world of gratitude for your encouragement and support. A warm hug to my amazing agent, Rosemary Stimola, for making the magic happen. A round of applause for my editor, Jennifer Heddle, for her care and insight in putting it all together. And special thanks to my brother Dan, who read all my early efforts and lived to tell about it.

*T*he other girls are already warming up, stretching their legs in unnatural directions on the blue mats. Ms. Summers shoots me a tight-lipped scowl, and I mouth, "I'm sorry."

I hang my jacket on the rack inside the door and drop my bag on the tiled floor underneath. As I breathe in the spicy odor of muscle rub, the tension in my chest uncurls and my muscles tingle with anticipation. Another dreary day of high school slides from my shoulders like an overstuffed backpack. It's time to dance.

I weave among bodies dressed in a rainbow of leotards to an empty mat. Some of the younger girls look up and smile, but the older ones ignore me. Over the years I've gotten too many of the lead dance roles they've wanted.

I've been taking dance from Ms. Summers since I was three, as many as four classes a week. But it never feels like too much.

I barely have time to stretch before Ms. Summers lines us up for the first routine. The recital is a month away, but she's already barking at us. Rehearsing for recitals drives her to the edge. "Oribella, front row stage left. Gypsy, front row stage right. I've added some new choreography."

New moves—yes! Gypsy and I are taller than most of the other girls, but Ms. Summers always positions us in front: blond and brunette, cream skin and olive. Even though Gypsy would love to smother me with a warm-up mat, we look great side by side.

Gypsy crowds into my personal space. "Or-i-bel-la makes another dramatic entrance. I bet you'd just *die* if you weren't the center of attention."

If Gypsy's dark eyes weren't squinty with anger, she'd look stunning. Her almost-black hair is piled up in tousled curls, and her emerald leotard flatters her skin tones. With her looks, I don't know why she wastes energy hating me.

Ms. Summers cues us to begin. I feel bodies pulsing around me, but Ms. Summers is all I see. Her body snaps to the music, all rhythm and sharp angles. She danced on Broadway—until she tore her Achilles tendon. Now she's the best teacher in Iowa, and the waiting list to get into her class is pages long.

I attach my movements to hers, like Peter Pan's shadow. My thighs and calves burn, my chest heaves, but discomfort is my friend. I'm a beauty queen, a model, an actress—soon to be a star. A warrior princess.

Sweat slides down my neck and pools in the hollow between my breasts. My lungs are starving for air, but I control my breathing and ignore the sparks doing their own dance behind my eyes.

Ms. Summers arches her back; I arch mine farther. She cuts to the right; my cut is sharper. Her arms punctuate the air; mine are exclamation points! The music pulses through my arms and legs, my torso. She is the teacher; I am the dance.

When the music stops, exhaustion slams into me. My head drops, and I clutch my thighs. Air as sweet and sharp as lemonade pours into my lungs. Beyond my sweat-coated lashes, the room spins.

"Magnificent, Oribella! Simply magnificent!" Ms. Summers chirps. Her face and neck are painted with red splotches, and her hand is pressed against her flat chest. I pushed her. Made her work. I smile inside.

"Gypsy, your transitions simply are not crisp enough." Ms. Summers shakes a finger in her face. "Practice and concentration are the key, my girl. Practice and concentration."

Gypsy mutters something, but I'm breathing too hard to hear it. She brushes by, her eyes flashing with anger, but Ms. Summers is probably right. For the past few months, when Gypsy practices, her moves are halfhearted, as if her mind and body are in different rooms. She's been taking lessons as long as I have. Why waste all that time and money on classes if she's not going to put herself out there?

While Ms. Summers helps a short, chubby blond with a series of steps she obviously hasn't mastered, I keep moving to stay loose. My mind jumps ahead to the meeting Mom and I have with Ms. W at seven-thirty this evening. Ms. W has lined up a movie audition for me—she told Mom that much over the phone. But she's waiting to tell us the rest in person.

It's still hard to imagine big-budget movies being shot and cast here in Iowa. But two years ago the Iowa legislature passed a tax incentive to encourage filmmakers to come here. Since then, major movies like *South Dakota* and *Peacock* have been filmed in Iowa—smaller films, too—which is a major break for actresses like me. Maybe this is the part that will move my career beyond peanut butter commercials and mall promotions and into the real dance. And the sacrifices Mom has made for me will have been worth it.

When Ms. Summers claps for attention, I step into place and let the music take me again.

When the hour ends, I gulp some bottled water while the other girls collect their gear and leave. The easy part is over. My private lesson with Ms. Summers is the killer. The new competition routine she choreographed for me pushes me to the limit, but it exhilarates me, too. Too bad the Crowning Glory pageant doesn't have a talent division. I won't be able to showcase this dance until the Miss USA Teen Sweetheart this winter.

No matter how strenuous the group lesson has been, Ms. Summers expects me to go all out on my solo. I shake myself loose and fill my lungs with air. She won't be disappointed.

My muscles groan. The short break between lessons made them stiff and lazy. Too bad. I'll knock the laziness out of them. Control, focus, discipline—traits every great actress must have.

The first half hour passes quickly. As I practice my routine, Ms. Summers circles me, snapping directions and tapping her pointer on the floor. At six o'clock, my eyes seek out the clock. Thirty more minutes.

"Focus, Oribella," Ms. Summers hisses in my ear. "To lose concentration is to lose everything."

Lose? Not my style.

2

The sky is dusty blue by the time Mom and I pull up to the Whitehaven Academy. The Academy is in a three-story redbrick house about one hundred years old, which makes it about three years younger than Ms. Whitehaven. The modeling classes and Ms. W's office are on the first two stories. She and her daughter, Philomena, live on the top floor. Since Philomena and I are in the same grade, I suppose Ms. W is *a few* years younger than 103.

Philomena is plodding up the stairs as Mom and I walk in. Her thighs and calves bulge under cutoff navy sweatpants, and her shoulder muscles strain against her long-sleeved gray tee. Her drab brown hair has no shine or body and looks like somebody cut it with garden shears.

But she's a star athlete at Highland, so I guess looks aren't important to her.

Philomena whirls around with a guilty look like she's not supposed to be climbing the stairs in her own house. When she sees me, she winces. This is clearly an encounter she'd rather not have, but I'm not sure why. We're not enemies; we just don't orbit the same sun.

When Philomena pushes her ragged bangs away from her forehead, it's obvious her eyebrows are untouched by wax or tweezers. Not attractive. "Hello, Mrs. Bettencourt. Mother said you—and Oribella—have an appointment. She's waiting for you in her office." Philomena points at Ms. W's door, as if Mom and I haven't been here a thousand times.

Ms. Whitehaven's office is a shrine to organization. She motions Mom and me into the stiff-backed wooden chairs that have been bruising my derriere for the past fifteen years.

Ms. W folds her tall, ultraslim figure into a padded leather chair. Her black linen suit is as smooth as her marble desktop. And even though she's ancient, her face is striking, with high, prominent cheekbones and a strong chin. "Mrs. Bettencourt," Ms. W's voice rasps like shoes scuffing on the sidewalk, "lovely to see you, as always."

I practice my interview posture while Ms. W and Mom go through the small-talk ritual. Back straight, chin tucked, ankles crossed. Hands folded neatly in my lap. The Whitehaven Way.

What can they have to talk about? I've been attending Whitehaven Modeling Academy since birth. Mom says I was a natural even as a three-month-old. And though I "graduated" over a year ago, Mom is still paying back the money she borrowed for my years and years of lessons. So I don't complain even after an all-day photo shoot like the one last month for Zonkers Department Store that left my smile muscles paralyzed and my feet swollen to Bozo the Clown size. After a few hours encased in ice packs, I was as good as new.

Finally, Ms. W turns to me. "Oribella, your head shots look wonderful. The photographer captured some lovely poses. I've arranged an audition for you with Whirlwind Productions on Thursday, the twenty-fourth at four-thirty. They are interested in you for the part of the young princess."

I peek at Mom's appointment book. Three weeks from tomorrow! My brain is jumping and squealing for joy. She sends me a proud smile, and a web of tiny lines forms around her eyes.

"Apparently it's something of a modern-day fairy tale, and the casting director was entranced by your beautiful face and long, lovely hair. He was also impressed with your work in commercials." Ms. W smoothes her triple strand of pearls, and I know she's excited for me. A lady *does not* fidget with her accessories.

"The part is a minor lead. The teenage princess, Razzi, appears in the first third of the film and in several flashbacks." Ms. W pauses. "The adult Razzi will be played by Skylar Moon."

Skylar Moon! This is too perfect.

I hope the filming takes weeks and weeks—months and months.

Of course, Skylar will stay in a fabulous condo while we're shooting. When each day's filming is done, she'll invite Mom and me to come over and chill by her pool. While we sip icy blue drinks decorated with fruit kabobs and paper umbrellas, she'll fill us in on the latest Hollywood gossip. And Skylar will tell everyone that I'm the little sister she's always wanted.

As soon as the picture is finished, Skylar will fly Mom and me to southern California for a stay in her oceanside mansion. We'll spend our days shopping on Rodeo Drive and being pampered at the priciest spas. At night we'll hit the clubs, and Skylar will introduce me to all her friends as her little sister. Of course, the paparazzi will follow us everywhere to snap pictures of Hollywood's two biggest stars. By then Skylar and I will be inseparable, and she'll insist that I have a part in her next project.

"Here are your sides. You do remember what sides are?"

I rouse myself from my daydream. "The lines I need to memorize for the audition," I recite dutifully.

Ms. W nods her head. "Of course, you must not only memorize these three pages, but immerse yourself in the character." She slides the script across the table. Her expensively cut white hair sparkles like fresh snow. "I take it the twenty-fourth will work for both of you."

"Yes, Ms. Whitehaven." I sneak a glance at my nail polish as I open the folder to peek at the script. No chips. Whew! Ms. W is obsessed about flawless nails.

Mom leans over to look at the pages. After work she freshened her hair and makeup, but forehead creases peek from under her blond bangs. She's worn out from working two jobs and managing my career. "Oribella is thrilled with this opportunity. And we have your agency—and you personally—to thank."

Ms. W nods. "I have every expectation that Oribella will be selected for the part." Her cultured smile takes in both of us. "The Whitehaven Agency has high hopes for Oribella. High hopes."

I see myself, poring over my very own script, highlighting my very own lines. Mom and I will rehearse until I can say every line while turning cartwheels in my sleep. I'll be magnificent—the star she's groomed me to be. At the audition, the casting director will break into spontaneous applause—

"So the Friday evening after your audition is acceptable to you, Oribella?"

Ms. W's question yanks me back to reality. "There will be music and dancing, I imagine—an opportunity for you to relax and socialize with people your own age. You teenagers need a way to unwind."

Mom jumps in to rescue me. "I'm afraid you caught

Oribella daydreaming about her first movie. However, I know she'd be delighted to attend Philomena's party. Right, princess?"

Party? I'm supposed to go to a party thrown by Philomena? I can't imagine a more deadly way to spend an evening. What do I have in common with a hoard of sweaty jocks? Mom and Ms. W are staring, waiting for me to respond, but if I say yes, I'll be condemned to hours of torment.

"Of course, Oribella will need to be home by nine o'clock," Mom says smoothly. "As you well know, her numerous commitments require her to maintain a strict bedtime schedule."

I breathe a sigh of relief. Mom, you are my hero.

3

On Saturday morning, I have the final fitting for my Crowning Glory gown. The Crowning Glory pageant—the most prestigious teen competition in the Midwest—draws contestants from fourteen states. If I win, I'll be one of the favorites going into the Miss USA Teen Sweetheart in February. And the winner of the Teen Sweetheart receives a five thousand dollar cash prize, which Mom could use to recoup some of our expenses.

Normally, Mom would come with me to a fitting, but today she's working extra hours at Bonds to make up for next Friday when we'll be driving to the pageant.

The bell above the door of Mrs. Tran's shop jingles as I walk in. She's been designing my gowns forever, but every time I come here, it's like entering an exotic country. The air is heavy with the fragrant scent of cloves and other spices I can't name. Gorgeous silk fabrics drape the walls. Each jewel-colored bolt of cloth is covered with delicate, handpainted scenes.

"Oribella!" Mrs. Tran rushes from the back room and grabs my hands. "You are as beautiful as a lotus blossom." She reaches up and cups my face. Then her fingers slide down my back. "Like silken sunshine, your hair. So, so lovely."

My damp-from-the-shower hair is pulled into a low ponytail and I'm wearing baggy old jeans and a pale blue crewneck sweater that hangs to my knees, but I'm used to Mrs. Tran's wild compliments so I don't squirm too much. It's not her fault. Most people act like beauty is something I've *accomplished*. But it's no different than congratulating me for having eyebrows or a nose. I'd rather be praised for mastering a tricky dance step or earning a C—if that's possible—in math.

"Your gorgeous dress is ready." Mrs. Tran bobs her head and smiles, showing the gap between her front teeth.

She grasps my hand and tugs me through the curtains into her workshop. I step into a downpour of gowns swaying in the lazy breeze of a rattly black fan. They hang from ceiling pipes, curtain rods, and a wobbly clothing stand that looks as if it's about to collapse.

Mrs. Tran jerks on the tail of my sweater. "Take off, take off! Try on dress."

I strip down to my bra and panties. The weather outside is nippy with the first breath of fall, but in Mrs. Tran's workroom I'm as warm as fresh bread.

She thrusts a pair of muslin mittens at me. "You must cover your hands whenever try on this dress. Your mother, too. Otherwise, you leave finger smudges. Ruin beautiful silk."

I know better than to argue with Mrs. Tran. Her dresses are her babies, only slightly less important than her grandchildren.

"Now close your eyes," she says. "In one moment you will surprise yourself."

Fabric, cool and silky, slips over me like expensive lotion. When Mrs. Tran zips up the back, I know the gown is a perfect fit.

"Ahhh!" Mrs. Tran sighs. "You make the sunrise hide its face."

I gasp at my reflection in the wavy mirror. The floor-length gown flows like a silken waterfall from my bust to just above my toes. Tiny tucks cinch in my waist, making it look impossibly small. Below the waist, the tucks unfurl into a rippling skirt that's slim-fitting but loose enough to allow me to walk without ruining the lines of the gown. The opalescent fabric molds to my figure, making each of my curves shimmer. As I turn from side to side, the color changes from pale rose to mauve to the blue of an evening sky. The bodice is cut to show a hint of cleavage, and the silver chains sliding over my shoulders are so tiny they're almost invisible. Mom says no strapless gowns until I turn sixteen next year, but this is almost as good.

"It's perfect, Mrs. Tran! Better than perfect!"

I reach out to hug her, but she steps back and waggles her finger. "Nobody touches. Oil from skin will ruin the fabric. I will wrap in special tissue until you wear at the pageant." Her eyes sparkle as she looks me over. "Other girls should stay home. Nobody is more beautiful than you."

When she compliments me this time, I don't even blink.

Monday morning I wake up hoping I've miraculously skipped five days and it's Saturday. Instead I'm facing another week of high school dreariness. At Highland High I'm a disease nobody wants to catch. The girls hate me, the guys avoid me, and the teachers think I have a single digit IQ. It's hard to concentrate on my studies in the face of so much blind adoration.

Tolerating school is an effort under normal circumstances, but with Crowning Glory less than a week away, it's impossible. My pageant obligations and professional commitments are much more important to me than anything that happens inside Highland High. But the State of Iowa has a different opinion about school attendance. Since Mom hasn't expressed an interest in spending time in jail, I put in an appearance just often enough to keep her out of handcuffs.

My feet drag up the concrete steps to my daily encounter with gloom. The double front doors have been propped open either to let in the fall breeze or allow the smell of stale cafeteria grease to escape. I don't have much hope of either one happening. With a resigned sigh, I walk in.

Other students brush by me, laughing and calling to their friends. They huddle in the halls—joking, gossiping, mulling over the plots of last night's TV shows. At least that's what I assume they're saying from the random words I hear as I walk past. Sometimes I wonder what they'd do if I joined one of their huddles. But what would be the point?

A chorus of wolf whistles comes from a group of jocks lounging by the gym in their green-and-white letter jackets. I turn my face away so they won't see me blush until I realize the whistles aren't for me. A short, chesty redhead in a V-neck cheerleader sweater and thigh-high pleated skirt flashes them a brilliant smile and wiggles her hips. They applaud and whistle louder. "Don't do that unless you mean it!" one of them yells, and the redhead laughs.

As she sways over to talk to them, I brush aside a sting of envy. Girls like her are so relaxed around guys. But I don't have a clue how to talk to them.

If Dad had lived to see me grow up, he might have taught me the ins and outs of communicating with boys. But it's only been Mom and me for as long as I remember. And for as long as I remember, she's told me that a serious performer needs to have tunnel vision about her career. And guys have no place in the tunnel.

She's right, of course. My energy is channeled into

dance lessons, acting lessons, modeling lessons. And when I'm not learning or practicing, I'm promoting myself. Which leaves little time for school and none for friends or guys. I had a few girlfriends in elementary school, but they drifted away when my professional obligations kept me from participating in their playdates and sleepovers.

"Hey, Gypsy!" a female voice bellows. Two girls flatten themselves against the wall as Morgan Price, Gypsy's most obnoxious groupie, barrels toward us. Morgan has unwisely chosen overprocessed blond as this week's hair color. Half a tube of eyeliner surrounds her eyes, and her pudgy cheeks blaze from the exertion of shoving unwary students aside. Her too-tight neon orange shorts and body-hugging tee shriek *fashion-challenged.*

As Morgan charges through the crowd, the oversize lime-green satchel hanging from her shoulder thumps against her wide rear end like a warning drum. But even when she's close enough for me to see the lipstick smudged on her teeth, I walk straight ahead. At the last moment she veers to the left, jabbing at me with her elbow. I sidestep, and she's thrown off balance. Her purse slips from her shoulder and empties into the middle of the packed hallway. Morgan hits the floor, scrambling to save her cell phone, cosmetics, and other goodies before they're trampled.

As I walk away, the dismal hall seems a little brighter. And it doesn't dim a bit when Morgan calls, "Bitch!"

4

When I open my eyes Saturday afternoon, it takes me a minute to realize I'm in the back of our van on the way to the Crowning Glory pageant in St. Louis. One of the damp tea bags has slipped off my eye and is stuck to my cheek in a soggy lump. A quick check in the mirror shows me the morning puffiness is gone. Mom's beauty remedies rule.

Mom sees me in the rearview mirror. "There's my sleeping beauty. Feeling better?"

I wobble up front and drop into the passenger seat. "Groggy, but better. I guess I was too excited to sleep last night."

Mom pats my knee. "At fifteen, your skin bounces back. At thirty-six"—she pulls the skin on her cheek—"not so much."

"You're beautiful, Mom. The best-looking mom at every pageant." She is, too, in spite of the "famous" nose she hates but has never been able to fix. Mom was raised by her grandparents, farmers who wouldn't spend money on "such foolishness," and she says Daddy didn't want her to change the face he loved. After he died, she used his life insurance for a down payment on our house, and she works two jobs to keep us going. But when my movie money rolls in, the first five thousand dollars is reserved for her nose.

Mom is convinced her nose is hideous. It's on the long-ish side with kind of an odd-looking bump on the bridge. But it's far from being hideous, and the rest of her features are striking. I have no doubt that Mom's obsession is connected to her mother, Arianna, who died when Mom was sixteen.

Great-Grandmother Eva says I look just like Arianna, which she means as a compliment. She says people who knew my grandmother still talk about how beautiful she was. But nobody ever says Arianna was a good person. When she was seventeen, she took the family car and drove to California to become a movie star. A year later she came back by bus—she'd sold the car—with my mom ready to pop into the world. Arianna wouldn't say who the father was, just that Mom got "his famous nose" and "it looks better on him than it does on you." She even nicknamed Mom "Beaky," which was supposed to be cute, but sounded mean.

Arianna stayed in Iowa just long enough to give birth to Mom and raid her parents' savings account. Once in a while Mom received postcards and letters describing Arianna's exciting life in Hollywood. And Arianna always called to let them know when she had a bit part in a movie. But she only came to visit Mom twice in sixteen years. Mom doesn't talk about it much, but I know she was crushed that Arianna didn't want her own daughter to be part of her life.

According to Great-Grandmother Eva, whenever people saw Mom all they talked about was Arianna, the Hollywood actress. It didn't matter that most of Arianna's parts were walk-ons with no lines. In a small town, even that was a big deal. But every time someone asked about Arianna, being left behind hurt Mom all over again. And every time someone gushed about Arianna's dazzling looks, Mom felt that much worse about her distinctive nose.

"Thank you, princess. Only twenty miles to the motel."

"I slept for hours! You should have woken me up to keep you company."

"I found an oldies station on the radio." She pats the faded dashboard. "And it's important that you look fresh when we check in—"

"Because you never know when the judges will be watching," I say along with her, and we giggle.

"Now tidy your hair and makeup. And slip into something that's not so rumpled." She checks the signs along the freeway. "People, get ready to meet the next Miss Crowning Glory."

Mom and I wrestle our luggage through the revolving door into the hotel lobby. Like every lobby I've ever walked into, it's heavy with recycled air and the sticky-sweet smells of hair gel and perfume. We trek past at least a hundred girls and their mothers—and enough suitcases to pave the interstate—to the front desk. Before Mom opens her mouth, the snotty girl behind the desk waves us away. "Pageant check-in is over there. Get in line."

"Lovely child," Mom mutters as we drag our suitcases to the other end of the lobby. "A shoo-in for Miss Congeniality."

I sink my teeth into my lower lip to keep from laughing.

The Crowning Glory sign is hanging above a shaky-looking card table. Despite all the people bumping into each other in the lobby, there's no line. If all these girls have checked in, why aren't they in their rooms getting ready?

As usual, Mom takes charge. "Oribella Bettencourt, age fifteen. We're entered in Photogenics, Loveliest Locks, Outfit of Choice, and—of course—Miss Crowning Glory."

The young woman sitting at the card table flips through a box full of pageant packets. She's gorgeous, with sunset-red hair and flawless makeup. I'm glad she's working the pageant instead of competing.

"I've found your registration," Welcome, My Name Is Margaret says. "Everything looks fine. But there's been a mix-up with the rooms." Her voice drops. "They won't be ready until three o'clock, which is why all these contestants are waiting in the lobby."

"I see." I know this news must have Mom freaking, but she keeps cool. "My daughter's interview was scheduled for three-fifteen. Has it been rescheduled?"

Margaret swallows. She's been asked that question a hundred times today, and not one person has liked the answer. "I'm afraid not. Our schedule is very tight."

"I'm sure it is. Coordinating a pageant is exhausting." Mom pulls some dollar bills from her purse. "Princess, run and get Margaret something to drink. Would you like soda, a water?"

I take the money and make eager-to-please eyes at Margaret. Mom and I have this routine timed to the second.

Margaret shakes her head, and her shoulders relax. That's probably the first nice thing anyone's said to her all day. "That's sweet, but I have a cooler of drinks under the table."

"If you're positive—" Mom steps around the card table and lowers her voice. "Margaret, you won the Crowning Glory two years ago. Right?"

Margaret's cheeks glow as she smiles and nods. Mom's knowledge of pageant trivia is amazing.

"You know how important it is to be rested for the

interviews. Not funky from eight hours in a van." Wrinkling her nose, Mom fans the shoulders of her sweater.

Margaret chuckles, and I know she's under Mom's spell. Someday, when I'm tired of competing, Mom should write a book revealing her secrets for charming pageant officials.

"I was wondering how it would work to allow the girls with the earliest interviews—say, from three to four o'clock—to move into the rooms that are clean and ready now? It might involve shuffling some room assignments, but . . ." Mom lets the sentence hang, and I know what's coming.

"But it wouldn't be that difficult, and it would be fair for everyone. Why didn't somebody here think of that?" Margaret's eyes light up. "Let me run and talk to the pageant coordinator. I'll be right back." She dashes across the room.

Mom turns to me and winks. "I think Margaret's about to move up the pageant ladder."

5

Pageant interviews are such a waste. I'd rather dance than answer a list of pointless questions, but not many pageants have talent competitions anymore. I think the judges got tired of watching girls with no talent embarrass themselves.

Thanks to Mom—and Margaret—I had plenty of time to get ready and rehearse my answers. Contestants aren't given the questions ahead of time—so we can be taken by surprise. But every interview is the same. Sometimes I'd like to sneak a tape recorder into the room and press the playback instead of answering. It would be fun to see the judges' faces when they hear the taped responses to their "surprise" questions.

My future? I'm going to devote my life to bringing about

world peace, eliminating poverty, and finding a cure for stupid questions.

The interview's not even so much about saying what the judges want to hear. It's about how you say it and how you look saying it. While I pretend to be thoughtfully considering their lame questions, they're examining me pore by pore. I sit with my ankles crossed and my hands resting in my lap. My back is Ms. W straight. My chin is up, but my eyes are the tiniest bit downcast to show respect for my elders.

We're in one of those hotel conference rooms with no windows and lots of bad air. If I ever interview somewhere that doesn't smell like feet, my nose will send a thank-you card. The walls are drab; the carpet is drab; the lighting is drab. My mission is to make the room glow with my presence.

The five judges sit behind a fake wood table scarred with coffee cup rings and cigarette burns. There are three women and two men, but to me their faces are computer screens filled with information: encouraging smiles, frowns of concentration, the dreaded glazed eyes of boredom. And I'm the well-programmed robot, responding to each command.

When a judge asks me a question, I look her—or him— in the eye. As I answer, I make eye contact with each judge in turn, beginning and ending with the judge who asked the question. I look thoughtful, I smile, I even laugh—but never giggle—at the lame jokes the men always make.

What do I want to be when I grow up? *An internationally famous actress and supermodel.* That's the perfect answer for anyone wanting to commit pageant suicide. I want to be a teacher, a role model, a mentor to children from deprived backgrounds. I want to make a difference.

If I could have one wish, what would it be? *To be adored and envied, and to be able to afford anything I want.* Not hardly. I wish people from all cultures and religions would come to understand and appreciate each other's uniqueness and diversity.

And so on, and so on.

If the casting director saw my interview technique, he'd serve me the role of Razzi with a side order of instant fame. And Mom and I would be set for life.

The interview lasts fifteen minutes, long enough for the judges to make sure I can put a complete sentence together. The one on the left checks me out for zits and visible signs of plastic surgery, which is not supposed to be allowed, but girls do it all the time. The unspoken rule is it's fine as long as nobody in the audience can tell.

"Thank you, Miss Bettencourt," the head judge says to let me know the interview is over.

I stand, then step up to shake each one's hand in turn. Their eyes widen with surprise. Then they smile. So nice—and such a joy—to meet a respectful young lady.

Before I walk out, I say, "Thank you for this opportunity to share my hopes and dreams."

The interview is a lock.

Backstage is pandemonium—the perfect setting for Mom and me. Like every pageant I remember, one-third of the moms and girls are crying, one-third are fighting, and the rest are in transition between the two. Most of the girls have competed before, but they still don't get it.

After fourteen years of pageants, Mom and I are like synchronized swimmers. Hair, makeup, ensemble; hair, makeup, ensemble. In the past four years we haven't lost a tube of mascara or an acrylic nail. Other girls are tear-streaked and frazzled; I'm the Queen of Composure.

My hair is down for the Loveliest Locks segment. When I step under the lights, the audience bursts into wild applause. Their adoration coats me like stardust. My blond waves brush the shoulders of my aqua dress suit as I twirl and strut, and the bias-cut skirt fans out above my knees. The crowd is still cheering as I bounce off stage and into Mom's arms.

"The judges are impressed with you," she whispers. "Even number four, who has been half asleep most of the evening, is all smiles."

Excitement sets me on fire. A win here will give me exposure throughout the Midwest—maybe the whole country.

Mom hustles me to the part of backstage we've claimed.

The air is syrupy with hair spray and nerves. All around me dresses puddle to the dirty floor, but she hangs my suit neatly in a garment bag. "Think of the dry-cleaning bills." She says the same thing at every pageant.

I hold out my hands, one at a time, so that Mom can wrestle with my above-the-elbow gloves. They're a pain to pull on, but when I'm wearing them, I feel as elegant as royalty. Then I raise my arms, and the opal gown flows over me. The cool silk caresses me. My hands smooth over the fabric, but my gloved fingertips feel nothing. How strange to wear a dress I can't touch.

Mom ties a muslin bib around my neck and retouches my makeup with expert hands. I stand motionless—Cinderella to her fairy godmother—and let the sable brushes dance over my cheeks.

Mom sweeps my hair up in both hands and swirls it on top of my head. "You're shedding, princess." My eyes fly open as a string of blond hair drifts to the floor. "Just like me," she says with a smile. "I shed every fall, too."

Mom slides the pins in my hair, barely grazing my scalp. She steps back and studies me from head to toe. "Breathtaking, princess. Tonight belongs to you."

"To us, Mom." Light as powder, I touch my cheek to hers.

In seconds the judges will make the final announcement. I won Loveliest Locks, placed second in Outfit of

Choice, and got the top score in Photogenics. But the gown competition and interview count 50 percent of the final score. What if someone else gave better phony answers than mine?

Shoulders back, head up, smile—only four teeth showing. The lights blind me, but I feel the audience, the judges. The auditorium hums with their energy.

The girl on my left is trembling so much that the front of her burgundy gown wobbles where her knees are knocking. She almost trips as she steps up for her third runner-up sash and tiara.

The second runner-up steps forward. Now it's me and the tiny brunette. She's adorable and bubbly, with killer dimples and wide brown eyes; her sleek chestnut hair covers her shoulders like a cape. Mom said she got a strong crowd reaction. The brunette and I slide together and hold hands. Her fingers are ice. Mine are almost too stiff to bend.

For a fraction of a second, I wonder why I endure this torture. Is an aluminum crown set with cubic zirconium worth the tooth-whitening treatments, facials, tanning-mist sessions, near-starvation diet, and my pricey pageant wardrobe? The heart-stopping anxiety of waiting to know if I've won?

"And now, the moment we've all been waiting for," the judge intones. "The selection of this year's Miss Crowning Glory. Miss Crowning Glory embodies the ideals of poise, beauty, and grace. But—most of all—she has tresses to delight the eye. A woman's hair is her Crowning Glory."

He opens the envelope with a flourish and turns to the brunette and me. Blood roars in my ears. His mouth moves, but the roaring drowns out his words. My breath comes in clumsy little puffs.

The tension shatters. The other competitors swarm me with awkward hugs and air kisses. Last year's winner slips the tiara into my hair. A sash skims over my head and settles across my shoulder. Flashbulbs explode in my eyes.

Relief overwhelms me. Then comes a swell of joy so intense that I feel as if I'm floating above the stage. Through a sheen of tears I see Mom at the edge of the curtains. Her hands are clasped under her chin, and she's laughing and crying. I blow her a kiss.

"Miss Crowning Glory—Oribella Bettencourt!" The judge touches my arm. "You won," he whispers. "Take your walk."

I turn toward the runway lights, and the crowd embraces me.

Yes, this is definitely worth it.

6

*B*ecoming Miss Crowning Glory sets my career on the fast track.

Ms. Whitehaven calls Monday morning while I'm getting ready for school. "Congratulations, Oribella. Your pictures are all over the Internet, and everyone wants you. I've booked you for three modeling appointments just this week. And The Fashion Edge, that trendy new boutique in the East Village, wants you for a series of holiday commercials." Ms. W stops to clear her nicotine-filled lungs. "But you mustn't neglect rehearsing for your audition."

"Of course not, Ms. Whitehaven." Like I'm not counting the seconds until then.

As soon as I've thanked Ms. W, I put Mom on the phone so she can enter the information into her Black-

Berry. While they're talking, I dance around my bedroom, dizzy with happiness. Three modeling assignments in one week! Not just one commercial—a series of them!

"Okay, Miss Whirling Dervish," Mom says when she hangs up the phone, "come in for a landing." She pats my comforter to invite me to sit. "You're much in demand, princess. We have a sleepwear shoot tomorrow afternoon for Jason Pierce, an informal on the *At Home with Roberta Show* Thursday morning, and another catalog shoot for Zonkers on Friday. That one will probably take all day."

Modeling and missing school—the perfect combination. Informals are fun because all I have to do is strut around onstage in a cute outfit for a minute while somebody describes what I'm wearing. Informals pay well, too. So does Zonkers.

"Why are we bothering with the Jason Pierce shoot, Mom, when they only pay in clothing? I already have more pajamas than I can wear."

Mom pats her hair. Her new layered cut and the highlights framing her face bring out her cheekbones and intense blue eyes. "Because a mail-order distributor like Jason Pierce gives you Internet exposure, which is priceless. And, we can sell the pajamas on eBay."

eBay? Are we that strapped for money?

Entry fees for Crowning Glory were over five hundred dollars, the wardrobe was more than two thousand, and Mom had to take Friday off without pay. "Can you afford to take more time off work to go with me?"

"I've been planning for several weeks to quit cashiering at Butterfly Boutique. The pay isn't worth the hours I have to work. Now that your career is catching fire, I have an excuse." She tucks a strand of hair behind my ear. "At Bonds, Fred will let me put in my hours evenings and weekends. That's the great thing about computers—I can work anywhere, anytime."

When she smiles, purple half-moons swell beneath her eyes. Her skin is gray with weariness. All because of me. "You're the world's most fabulous mom."

"And I expect you to shower me with expensive gifts when *you're* fabulously wealthy." She throws back her head, fluffing her hair like a model at a high-fashion shoot.

Then Mom's expression turns serious, and she takes my hands. "Sometimes I worry that all this is putting too much pressure on you. That *I'm* putting too much pressure on you."

I roll my eyes. "We had this conversation last month. You're not putting pressure on me. I love my life. And I'm not going to stop now just when we're getting to the good part." I squeeze her hands. "So quit worrying and enjoy it."

"You're sure?"

"I'm sure." Mom has worked two jobs—sometimes three—and gone without things she needed so I could have a perfect life.

When I was a kid, I took my expensive pageant wardrobes and recital costumes for granted. I was too wrapped up in myself to notice that Mom was wearing the same outfits year after year. And I never gave it a thought when Mom sat through recital practices that lasted until midnight after she'd worked all day. The next morning she'd be up before I was, doing laundry and cooking breakfast while I whined about having to get out of bed. On the weekends she drove me all over the state to modeling cold calls and kept me entertained while we waited hours for an audition.

What a selfish witch I'd be to complain now that her sacrifices are paying off.

Mom's face lights with relief. She jumps up and pulls me to my feet. "Go finish getting ready, princess. We leave in three minutes."

I'm going to wear my hair half up and half down today. With the top pulled back from my face, it's a "beauty queen casual" look. My shedding phase must be over because there's nothing in my brush but two stray hairs.

Mom and I are a breath away from getting everything we ever wanted.

Spanish could not be more boring. Every day is the same: ten minutes of watching a language video, ten minutes of parroting Mr. Frontino's conversational Spanish, and one tedious worksheet.

While I'm pretending to recite with the rest of the class, I doodle stage names around the margin of my worksheet. *Ori Bettencourt—star of stage, screen, and . . . Bella*

Bettencourt—actress, model, and . . . Ori Bella—don't think so. Sounds like an overweight belly dancer. Besides, Mom would throw a fit if I shortened my first name, especially since Daddy chose it. When I'm freakishly famous, I won't need a last name.

Flashbulbs explode in my face as I step from my white Mercedes limousine onto the red carpet. I pose and smile for the paparazzi, trying not to feel too smug that at age seventeen I've been nominated for my third Academy Award. After winning an Oscar for Best Supporting Actress in Razzi's Tale, *I went on to win Best Actress for my role in my second movie,* She Walks in Beauty—*the only actress to win Oscars for her first two movies. According to the Hollywood columnists, I'm about to make it three in a row.*

I lift the hem of my sleek black gown, which shows off my celebrated blond hair and pale skin to perfection. The high neckline drapes just above my collarbones and flows down my back, which is daringly low cut. I've chosen to wear my hair up in an artful disarray of curls held in place with a string of diamonds. My strappy silver shoes are studded with diamonds to match my hair and earrings.

Mom walks by my side, wearing a stunning red gown. Thanks to a series of Botox and Juvéderm treatments, she looks ten years younger. Her nose—fashioned by the cosmetic surgeon Skylar recommended—is a work of art.

A handsome man in uniform signaling us from behind the velvet rope catches my attention. He's tall and slender with blond hair and green eyes exactly like mine. My heart skips a beat because he can't possibly be who he seems. But when he smiles, my doubts disappear. It's Dad, alive after all, wearing his National Guard uniform and looking just like he did in the last picture Mom took of him.

Mom and I cry out with joy and rush to hug him. Dad ducks under the rope and embraces us, and my heart soars with perfect happiness. He offers each of us his arm, and the three of us walk up the red carpet together.

I blink away tears as Mr. Frontino announces the "checking our worksheets" part of class. *Trabaja de oficinista.* He works as a clerk. *Se subio al tren.* He got on the train. *Se ha ido a casa.* He has gone home. Lucky guy.

Lunch is an ordeal I can do without, and I have tried every way to escape. Library, no food allowed; outdoors, ankle-deep construction mud; locker room, nauseating; restroom, beyond nauseating; empty classrooms, where teachers hide to avoid us. But skipping food is impossible. My blood sugar dips and turns my complexion sallow. Not a look the camera loves. So I endure.

I assume my runway stance and shoulder past the guys who are forever lurking in the cafeteria doorway. As always, they gawk. And, as always, I look straight ahead and pretend not to notice the waves of testosterone sloshing over me.

"Hi." The muscular junior that Gypsy and her crowd regularly gush over steps forward. I think his name is

Derrick. He smiles and touches his forehead in a little salute. Derrick has nice eyes and strong cheekbones. Before it dawns on me that it would be polite to say hello, I've passed him. Only someone more socially inept than I am—if that's possible—would turn back now.

If Derrick were a pageant judge or photographer, I'd know what's expected. But suppose I said hello and Derrick ignored me or laughed in my face? What's the right way to deal with that? If a guy stares at my chest, do I slap him or pretend I don't notice? Other girls seem to know the rules, but I can't sort it all out.

I spot a corner table with three girls sitting on one end and slide into a chair with empty seats all around. I need a few minutes alone with my carrot sticks and yogurt. A pain has been pulsing behind my eyes all morning.

Trays hit the table on all sides of me. "Hey, Oribella. Is this section reserved for beauty queens or are lowly humans like us allowed here, too?"

A groan travels from my toes to the top of my head. Not Gypsy and her traveling band of bitches. "It's a free table." I shove a carrot stick into my mouth and wonder how long I'd have to hold my breath to turn invisible.

"So, what was last weekend's pageant?" Gypsy raises her voice so everybody within twelve tables can hear. "Miss Stuck-up America? Miss Superficial USA? Miss I'm-Too-Beautiful-To-Be-Human?"

Carrot chunks lodge in my throat, but I wash them down with bottled water and scoop the remains of my lunch into my bag. I could mention how Gypsy used to go to Ms. W's Academy, too, until she was kicked out because her parents didn't pay their bills. I know because I *happened* to see some papers on Ms. W's desk. But throwing that tidbit in Gypsy's face would mean sinking to her subhuman level.

As I push my chair back, Gypsy blocks it with her foot.

"I get it. You don't like me, you don't like pageants, you don't like blonds, whatever." I lift the chair over her foot and squeeze out. "So ignore me. I'll try to endure the pain of your rejection."

Gypsy's face is the color of a bad sunburn. As I walk away, her eyes burn laser holes into my back.

Three more classes to survive before I escape high school purgatory. Maybe I can do the rest of tenth grade online.

7

Early Tuesday morning I tiptoe into Mom's bedroom and close the blinds and curtains so not the tiniest ray of light will slip in. She's flat on her back with one of her horrible migraine headaches. Her eyes are squeezed shut, and her hands press against her temples. My heart hurts to see her in so much pain.

I slip out of her room and scurry downstairs. According to her BlackBerry, she's working both jobs again today. For now I'll just call Bonds and tell them she won't be in. If she's not feeling better by this afternoon, I'll have to call Butterfly Boutique, too. Mom will be upset about losing all that pay.

While I'm in telephone mode, I call school to tell them I won't be in. My Mom impression isn't the best, and I hear skepticism in the secretary's voice. No big deal; Mom will write me an excuse note tomorrow. I'm a horrible person to feel even the tiniest bit happy about Mom being miserable, but . . . no mind-numbing classes, lunchroom horror, or harassment by Gypsy's gang. Bliss.

Now that I've freed up the day for us, I can concentrate on Mom. I grab an ice pack from the fridge and wrap it in a dish towel. I make up a pitcher of ice water, grab a tumbler and her pills, and stack everything on a tray. Nurse Oribella to the rescue.

Mom hasn't moved. I ease the tray onto her bedside table and touch her gently on the shoulder. When her head's pounding, she can't bear one decibel of sound. She started having migraines just after I turned fourteen, and they got so bad that for a while she was having one every two or three weeks. But last May she saw a specialist who put her on new medication. When she went five months without a single migraine, we hoped she was finally over them.

"Oh, princess, I feel so awful," she moans. She opens her eyes a slit, groans, and covers them with her hands. Her face is shiny with sweat, and she's holding herself so still that I know it hurts her just to breathe.

I help Mom sit up and take her pill, then lower her onto the pillow and smooth back her hair. With a touch lighter than dandelion fluff, I settle the ice pack on her forehead. She sighs.

"Sit next to me and hold my hand, princess."

I move her vanity chair to the bed and take her hand, stroking it the way I would an injured bird. The back of her hand is plump and soft, but her palm is sticky.

"You shouldn't stay home to take care of me." Her voice is raspy, and I lean close to hear her. "But the pain . . ." Tears trickle from the corners of her eyes.

"I wish I could take it away." My eyes mist over as I soak up her tears with a tissue. "When I land that movie role, you'll do nothing but relax and get massages from hunky guys. No more working and no more headaches."

Mom's flowery perfume doesn't quite mask the tangy sourness of her sweat. She hasn't thrown up—yet—but I gauge the distance to her wastebasket just in case.

The corners of her mouth curve a little. "That's a lovely thought, princess," she murmurs, "but I've never had the looks to attract hunky guys." When Mom has a migraine, she usually doesn't want to talk, but sometimes it distracts her from the pain.

"Not true." I hate the way she puts herself down. "Guys look at you all the time. Besides, Dad was a hunk, and he fell in love with you."

"Lee was sweet and funny and loving and an absolute genius with numbers, but he wasn't what most girls would consider a hunk." Mom stirs a little and yawns.

"Sweet and funny and loving are the best kinds of hunky. And Daddy's face had character, which is much better than boring old handsome." I've pored over his pictures so many times that I have his face memorized, but—

except for our eye color and the shape of our noses—I look much more like Mom than Dad.

Mom lets out a long breath. "You're right, princess. Much better. I wish so much that you could have known him."

"Me, too." *Every day of my life.* "Okay, that's enough girl talk for now." Being sad isn't going to make Mom feel better. "Time for you to rest." I stand up and smooth the covers around her.

"What would I do without you?" Her words are slurring; the medicine is working.

"I'm right here, Mom. Always right here."

8

$\mathcal{M}$odeling is exhausting, but it has its benefits. Makeup artists and stylists fuss over me. The wardrobe people dress me in one stunning outfit after another. And it's perfect acting practice. What expression do you want: Pouty? Surprised? Delighted?

I was up this morning before six to wash my hair, set it on rollers, and blow it dry. Whenever possible, I avoid using a curling iron. Split ends are not attractive under any circumstances. Before a modeling shoot I put on a light foundation and a layer of mascara. The makeup people on site take care of the rest.

Ron, the photographer, is a skinny guy who looks like he's barely out of high school. He has a wispy blond mustache and spotty chin hairs that cannot in any way be called a beard. But Ron's one of the nicest photographers I've worked with. He doesn't smoke or swear or act like he's too good for catalog work. And he compliments us all the time, even the little kids who scratch their bottoms when he's trying to get a shot.

Lots of actresses got their start posing for catalogs. Someday the hosts of *Before They Were Famous* will show these pictures to the audience. "It's true, folks. Before she won her six Academy Awards, Oribella posed for the Zonkers catalog in Des Moines, Iowa."

"Okay, girls, you're best friends on a holiday vacation at the beach, telling each other secrets. Let me see some giggly best friend action."

Best friends. What would that be like? We'd eat lunch together, walk to classes side by side, and talk on the phone every night for hours even if we'd spent the whole day together.

Could I be friends with this nameless girl standing beside me? She looks younger than I am, but round-faced girls tend not to look their age. Although she's a few inches shorter, we're close enough in height that we'll photograph well together. Her hair is golden brown and cut in a classic bob with straight bangs that fall just above her eyebrows. But her large, amber eyes are by far her best feature.

I turn to her and bubble over with giggles. She giggles back, showing a gap between her front teeth. But when I try to make eye contact, she's looking over my shoulder.

Focus, Oribella. You're here to do a job—not make friends.
And how would a friendship with another model work out the
first time you and she competed for the same shoot?

Ron jumps around us, snapping pictures and telling us
how great we look. As soon as he's finished, we break apart
and get ready for the next shot.

After a quick change into tan corduroy pants, a red
scrunch-neck sweater, and a slouchy faux fur hat, I'm
standing by the fireplace drinking eggnog with four of
my closest non-friends. This time I keep my eyes straight
ahead and my mind on the role I'm playing. The hat
itches, and the boots I'm wearing are half a size too small,
but I'm used to that. It's superhot under the lights, but at
least we're shooting the winter catalog in October instead
of cooking in the blazing July sun.

When we're finished, I grab a drink of water from
the bottle in my bag. I rub the stiff muscles in the back
of my neck and stretch my jaw. My cheeks are sore from
smiling.

"You're pretty."

A girl with fiery red hair whose head barely reaches
my chest is gazing up at me. She's wearing a blue, ruffled
dress that makes her look like a baby doll. I'd guess she's
four or five. "Your hair's like Rapunzel—you know, in the
fairy tale. Can I touch it?"

"Sure, if you want to." I tip my head to the side, and
she pets my hair in long strokes like it's a horse's mane.
Her eyes are bright blue, and her face is blotchy with

freckles. In a few years she'll hate them, but now she's darling. "You're pretty, too."

Before I find out her name, one of the photographer's assistants snatches her away.

"Bell, is it?" It's photographer Ron. Beads of sweat hang on his scrawny mustache like leftovers from a sneeze.

"Oribella." Would it be too weird if I handed him some tissues?

"Yeah, okay." He scratches his head under the baseball cap he's wearing backward. "We've decided to put you in some more shots. Go to hair, then wardrobe."

More shots! Every photo means more money and less pressure on Mom. If I weren't a professional, I'd bound across the floor like a kangaroo.

I wish she were here, but she's working both jobs today. I helped her eat some soup around eight o'clock last night, but when she drove me here this morning, she still had massive dark circles under her eyes.

Bev, the stylist, is a stocky lady with a sour-pickle face who acts like fixing hair is her least favorite thing in the world. Her palms are covered with thick, snaggy calluses.

Bev snatches my hair into a ponytail and drags a brush through it. Tears spring into my eyes. My shoulders bunch as I wait for her next assault on my snarls. Instead, Bev lets my hair drop.

"Something's wrong, girl." Bev calls all the models "girl" or "boy." She dangles a clump of hair in front of my face. "Your hair should not be coming out like this."

You jerked so hard, I'm surprised my head stayed on! "Mom says I'm just shedding a little hair. Because it's fall."

Bev shuffles around until we're eye to eye. "Fall, schmall. This"—she shakes the blond clump—"is not a 'little hair.' Losing a bunch of hair like this is *not* normal." Bev drops my hair into my lap. "You need to get this checked out by a doctor. There's not much work for bald models."

9

*B*ev scares me silly.

For the whole next week I'm terrified to touch my hair. I baby it in the shower—one tiny droplet of shampoo and a fistful of conditioner. After school I shop the mall for the widest-toothed comb ever invented. I skim the comb through my slick, wet hair with my eyes closed tight. I hold my breath until silver spots flash across my eyeballs. Then I peek, one slitted eye at a time, to see how much hair is in the comb. I only start breathing when I see it's practically empty. On my hands and knees in the shower, I pick through yucky soap scum in search of follicles stuck in the drain. Instead of the tight twist I usually wear for dance class, I coax my hair into a knot on the back of my neck, so loose it falls out halfway through class and Ms. Summers snarls and hisses until I refasten it.

My biggest acting challenge isn't immersing myself in the role of Razzi. It's not letting Mom see how scared I am. She's had two killer migraines since Crowning Glory; this would blow the top of her head off.

Whatever I'm doing works, because only eighty or so hairs sneak out each day, which—according to my Internet research in the school library—is perfectly normal. Every morning I inspect my scalp for bald patches, but I can't even find the place where the clump of hair fell out. The tight band around my chest relaxes, and my stomach stops squirming. Now I can concentrate on becoming a star.

The scene I'm rehearsing for the audition comes just as Razzi—who's a fairly normal teenager—is confronted outside her apartment building by two guys who have been stalking her for the past few days. The men unroll a document that says the future king of Yorlanot has commanded Razzi to attend his coronation. To be held in his mysterious kingdom across the sea, of course.

Memorizing the lines is the easy part. The hard part is getting into Razzi's head, not just imagining, but *knowing* how she feels—and why she says what she says—when two stalker weirdos tell her to pack her nightie and get ready to travel because she's the king's long-lost baby sister.

The sensible reaction would be to kick the guys in the crotch and scream like a madwoman, but that's not in the script. So, obviously Razzi's not that kind of girl. She's strong and independent—and she thinks these guys are crazy—but she fights them with words and attitude instead of karate chops.

I spend a lot of my rehearsal time saying the words in my head with my eyes closed. I want to think Razzi's thoughts, understand what motivates her. Then I play the scene to Mom with the inflections and gestures that feel right, and she gives me feedback. She has wonderful instincts, which she probably inherited from Grandmother Arianna. If Mom's not convinced by my performance, nobody else will be. So far, she hasn't been convinced.

No wonder I'm eating aspirin like they're Tic Tacs.

One fun part of preparing for my audition is putting my outfit together. Mom and I pore through catalogs and magazines in search of a "modern-day princess" look. When I'm not at dance class, rehearsing, or on a modeling shoot, we haunt funky little shops for dresses and accessories. I'm about to despair when Mom finds a sleek ivory dress with three rows of tiny pearls around the scooped neckline. The sleeves taper at the wrists, and the slightly flared skirt falls to just above my knees. We pair it up with a simple but elegantly fitted black jacket. After trying several different treatments at the waist, Mom and I decide it looks best without a belt. To add some drama to the look we choose peep toe three-inch heels the color of cayenne pepper. We experiment with different hairstyles—and I try to stay calm while

Mom is brushing and tugging. But whatever problem I had with my hair has vanished. A few days after we find the dress Mom comes home with an old pearl choker she unearthed at a vintage store. With the choker holding my hair off my face, the look is complete.

Going to school on audition day is unthinkable. I'm *so* close to grasping Razzi that I feel my consciousness twining around hers like a vine. I spend the morning fine-tuning my lines, giving her just the right amount of attitude, sassy but not over the top. The casting director has to see that I—nobody else—am Razzi.

Mom leaves work at eleven o'clock to help me run through my lines one last time. The first time we rehearsed my scene together, we fell apart giggling when she tried to make her voice sound like one of the king's tough guys. But today we're all business.

Before Mom and I run lines, we practice a variation on the visualization technique I use to focus myself before a complicated dance number. Only this time we're using it to bring Razzi to life.

"Princess, you know how Razzi thinks, you know what she wants, you know everything about her. Close your eyes and imagine that the world's greatest hypnotist is putting you under a spell." Sitting on the living room sofa, I let my eyes droop while Mom's voice lulls me. "Now take three long, deep breaths. With each breath Razzi is moving into your brain and body, becoming everything you think and say and do."

I slow my breathing and let the traffic noises, our rumbling old furnace, and even Mom's voice drift away. I imagine Razzi flowing into my lungs like an exotic perfume, filtering into every cell of my body. I see the way she smiles and frowns and walks; I hear her speak and laugh; I understand her thoughts and motivation. More deep breaths, and I picture myself at the audition delivering my lines perfectly. My voice captures every nuance of her character, and my body assumes her regal posture. With those images embedded in my subconscious mind, the last whispers of uncertainty evaporate.

One last deep breath, and I open my eyes. "Okay, Mom. I've got her. Let's try it."

When we've run through the scene one last time, Mom gives me a hug that lifts me off the floor. "That's it, princess! You're Razzi to her very core."

The afternoon is hair and makeup. Mom dabs concealer under my eyes and blends it in. She pats sheer foundation over my whole face—even my eyelids and lips—with a makeup sponge. Then she lightly pencils in my eyebrows, applies pearl-colored shadow to my brow bones, a streak of gray eyeliner along my lashes, and two coats of inky mascara. When my eyes are finished, she outlines my lips with dark rose and fills them in with glossy lipstick one shade lighter. She dots creamy blush on my cheeks and smoothes it along my cheekbones. After an hour she steps back to look at her handiwork. "The lighting is sure to be awful, but all the girls will be coping with the same conditions." She dusts my forehead and chin with the merest trace of powdered mineral blush. "And none of them will be as gorgeous as you."

Held back by the pearl choker, my hair cascades down my back in shiny golden waves. It looks thick, healthy, and perfect.

The Whirlwind Productions office is on the second floor of a building downtown. Ms. W said the company rented temporary space for casting. The building looks like it's been crumbling for the last three centuries and won't last much longer. Half of the gray stuff between the bricks is missing, and paint around the windows is chipping off.

Mom and I step into a clunky elevator that's contaminated with the aroma of armpits and foot fungus. As it fights to lift us to the second floor, it makes a horrible grinding noise. Mom rolls her eyes and says, "Come on, Old Bessie, don't fail us now!" and we're still laughing when the elevator door opens.

The office looks nothing like I'd imagined. The receptionist's "desk" is a cardboard table with giant stick figures scribbled on it in black marker. Her legs are stretched out to the side, showing off pricey distressed jeans. Her short black hair is artfully messy. But she's barking orders into a cell phone in a voice that's all business.

When Mom and I hesitate just inside the door, the woman circles her free arm in a *come on over* gesture. The sleeve of her purple sweater flaps, and dust swirls into the air.

"Mother, are you sure this is the right place?" I whisper. "Ms. W must have—"

The woman slaps her hand on the table. "Are you auditioning for Razzi? If not . . ." She jerks her thumb toward the door.

Three pretty teenagers, lined up like dolls at a tea party, sit on folding chairs. Like me, they have long blond hair. But, they're all wearing sparkly princess dresses with ruffles and flounces. One has her hair piled around a rhinestone-studded tiara. In their pastel pinks, blues, and greens, they look like wedding mints. Their mothers or agents sit next to them, fiddling and whispering.

What if Ms. W forgot to tell Mom we were all supposed to dress that way?

While I'm fighting off a panic attack, Mom rallies. She puts her palm in the middle of my back and guides me to the receptionist. "Oribella Bettencourt. She has a four-thirty audition."

"Yeah, yeah." Blackie waves her off. "As you can see, we're backed up here. The casting people just got off a conference call with Los Angeles," she says as she scrolls through her cell phone menu. "You're looking at a forty-five-minute wait—minimum."

Mom's neck breaks out in red blotches, but she bites

her lip. Arguing with Blackie would be pointless. We settle into the last two rusty folding chairs in the waiting room. Mom takes the chair next to the pink princess so that I'm on the end.

When I try to sit Ms. W style, the chair cuts into my rear. The room is stuffy, and Blackie is shrieking into her cell phone again. This shouldn't be getting to me. I've waited for a thousand interviews and modeling assignments, but this is different. This is my future.

Mom squeezes my hand. "Remember, princess," she whispers, "this is rented space. Their Los Angeles offices are probably fabulous." She lifts a curl over my shoulder. "And Ms. Whitehaven only deals with companies of the highest quality."

She's right, of course. Ms. W would never risk her agency's reputation by doing business with a company that wasn't top tier.

Mom puts her lips to my ear. "Relax, darling. These girls are lovely, but *you're* Razzi."

I close my eyes and smile.

After about twenty minutes, the door to the audition room creaks open. The girl who glides out knocks the wind out of me. She's taller than I am and has streaked blond hair that cascades below her waist. Her cheekbones are high and dramatic, her lips collagen pouty, and her eyes are an intense blue. A midnight-blue gown drapes across one shoulder and clings all the way to the floor, showing off a bustline that is a touch too large for her frame. But—enhanced or not—she's stunning.

As she walks past, I feel like a peasant gawking at a queen. How can I compete with someone so gorgeous and sophisticated? My confidence whooshes away.

But only for a second.

Not just any beautiful girl can be Razzi. Razzi has attitude; she's feisty and independent—the kind of girl who has to be dragged into an ivory tower kicking and screaming.

The noisy, musty room fades as Razzi grows inside my head. Her voice fills my mouth like the tang of a grapefruit. My hands tingle with her gestures. My spine straightens, and my leg muscles snap. When I stand, I will use her regal posture. When I walk, my legs will step with her determined stride. Razzi has possessed me.

10

After more than two hours of waiting, Mom and I are comatose. The sun has set, my derriere is numb, and the last pastel princess left the building fifteen minutes ago. Even Blackie has abandoned her cell phone. She's yawning while she turns the pages of a *People* magazine.

The door to the casting room opens a crack. "Anyone else?" a tired voice asks.

Blackie flips her wrist in our direction. "That one—Bittensomething."

The door opens the rest of the way, and a tall woman steps out. She's wearing a tight black sweater and jeans, and if she has any muscle, it doesn't show. Her bleached white hair is divided into a zillion braids that wriggle over her shoulders like snakes, but her roots are blood red. Black lipstick and eyeliner slant halfway to her ears.

I swallow a gasp. I thought that look was reserved for rock stars and zombies—not casting directors.

She sighs. "Come on in," she says, not even trying to hide her irritation. "It's late, and we've had a long day."

Mom gives the skinny woman a clenched-tooth smile and picks up her purse.

My poor leg muscles have frozen in the bent position, and I wobble to my feet. I try to summon Razzi, but I feel like a rusty tin soldier.

The zombie/rock star almost lets the door close in our faces, but Mom grabs it in time. Musty air hits me—cigar smoke, coffee dregs, and Old Spice-smothered body odor. The waiting room was a palace compared to this.

"Oribella Bettencourt," the man sitting behind the desk booms. The rest of us are drooping, but he's bristling with energy. "What a handle! I'll call you Bell." His face is round, and his hairline has receded to the back of his head. The hair that's left is pulled into a skinny gray ponytail.

He hoists himself up and captures my hand in both of his. "Martin Storm, casting director. You've met my assistant, Misty Woods." His hands are damp and squishy as a soggy washcloth. Mom holds out her hand for him to shake, but he won't let go of mine.

Martin Storm and I stand there hand in hand, like junior high kids on their first date. Misty Woods scowls, and I wonder if she's impatient, or jealous. Maybe Martin and Misty have a thing going. *When they have sex, is there a storm in the woods?*

"Okay, Bell, let's see what you've got." His squinty eyes slide over me, top to bottom and back up. "Great bone structure. Right build. And that hair—"

Martin Storm drops my hand and scuttles around the desk. My palm is wet and sticky, and I'm dying to wipe it on my skirt. Before I can, he's beside me. Gunk is crusted in the corners of his eyes, and he has foul coffee breath. Before my gag reflex kicks in, I let my eyes go out of focus and breathe through my mouth.

He grabs my hair in both hands and lifts it off my neck. My skin crawls, and I'd like to bring my heel down on his instep. But Razzi wouldn't, and neither will I.

Then he paws the back of my head and examines my roots. His fingers feel like sticky worms crawling along my scalp. I hold myself still, fighting every instinct telling me to push him away. "Now this is hair, Misty. Thick, gorgeous, natural blond." He buries his nose at the back of my head and sniffs. "Smells like flowers."

My hold on Razzi slips when Martin Storm starts patting me down like he's checking for concealed weapons. *How is this in any way part of an audition?* His smelly breath puffs against my neck, and his hands are dangerously close to places they shouldn't be. My flesh shrinks from his groping hands, but I have nowhere to run. In two seconds I am going to forget how important this part is and knee him in the crotch.

"Excuse me, Mr. Storm." Mom grabs his sleeve. "Oribella is here for an audition—to be seen and heard." She smiles, but her eyes are murderous. "If you're concerned about implants, as her mother I can guarantee that everything is genuine."

Martin Storm chuckles. "Good to know, ma'am." His hands reverse direction, creep up my neck, and burrow under my hair. He rakes his fingers up, pulling out Mom's carefully positioned pearl headband.

"Oops!" Storm holds up a skinny lock of my hair, and I almost faint. "Guess some goldilocks got caught on my ring. Sorry, babe."

"Marty, get your hands off that poor girl and let her read for the part," Misty says.

Read? How can I read when I can't even breathe? I send Mom a pleading look. She gives her head an almost invisible shake, and I know what she's thinking. *It doesn't matter how disgusting he is. Make him love you.*

Martin Storm drops my hair and wedges his broad rear end into his desk chair. "Okay, Bell. Dazzle me."

I take a deep, deep breath and summon Razzi. "I don't care what King Whatever's His Name has decreed! I will not attend his coronation." Storm's face fades away as he becomes one of the king's lackeys. "And why should I believe you—either of you?" I whirl on Misty Woods, lackey number two. "From what I see, you're nothing more than two strangers with phony accents and horrible taste in suits!"

On the drive home I pull a package of wipes from Mom's purse and rub them over my hands, face, and neck.

"He's a slimy little man, princess," Mom says, "but I stopped him before he crossed the line."

Maybe he didn't cross your line, but his hands were all over mine!

"And you charmed the socks off him. We'll get a call-back, I know it."

"I have to see him again?" If I hadn't digested lunch hours ago, I would lose it now.

"Probably more than once. For a big part like this, there may be several—" Her cell phone chimes. "Hello. Yes, Ms. Whitehaven. We just left. Very well, I thought."

I turn Mom off and stare out the car window. It's raining, and the streetlights look fuzzy through the streaked windows. I want to be a star; I have to be a star. All the disgusting Martin Storms in the world can't stop me.

But Mom doesn't understand what it feels like to be *inspected*, like a used car somebody is deciding whether or not to buy. I know she wouldn't let anybody hurt me, but tonight I need a hero.

"Daddy was a great guy, right?" I ask when she clicks her cell phone shut. Mom doesn't like to talk about Dad because it reminds her of how much she still misses him, but right now I need to feel him close to me.

"More than great. He was the kindest, most generous man." The streetlights play across her face like the frames of an old-fashioned black and white movie. "When we were first married, he'd bring me a little surprise almost every night."

"Like what?"

"A bright-colored scarf, an imitation pearl bracelet, a little toy squirrel that ran up and down the table leg—something to make me smile. As if he wasn't everything I needed. . . ." Her voice trails off.

"Tell me about when he named me."

"You've heard that story a thousand times."

"Please." Anything to keep her talking about Daddy.

Mom sighs, but she's smiling. "As soon as Lee and I found out you were going to be a girl, we started trying out names. I was determined we'd name you Eva—"

"—because it's your grandmother's name, and she and Great-Grandfather Bert raised you." I finish for her. "But Daddy said you should wait until you saw me."

"And he was right, as usual." She shakes her head.

"It stormed the entire night I was in labor—rain, thunder and lightning like the end of the world. You know how I hate storms, but with Lee beside me, holding my hand, I felt safer than safe."

Her eyes shine with tears.

"You were born just at sunrise, and when the nurse put you in Lee's arms, sunlight surrounded your head like a halo." Mom reaches across the seat and strokes my hair. "And Lee said, 'Ronnie, say hello to Oribella—our beautiful, golden child.'"

I imagine Daddy dressed in khaki pants and a blue shirt, holding tiny me. His arms are warm and strong, and I feel his heart beating against my side. He's whispering in my ear—father/daughter secrets nobody else will ever hear. His face is rough with stubble, and his eyes are drooping because he's been up with Mom all night, but his smile is like the sun because he loves me more than the world.

But my memories are all imagination because just after my second birthday, Daddy's National Guard unit was called to active duty. He drowned during a training exercise a week before they were going to be shipped overseas. If someone is insensitive enough to ask for details, Mom's lips get tight, and she shakes her head. But the pain in her eyes knocks the wind out of me.

Daddy would never have let Martin Storm touch me. But if Daddy were alive, I'd have grown up around computer geeks instead of models. What would he say if he saw me now?

"Tell me about how nervous Dad was when he gave me my first bath. Or maybe the time he took me to the park and the puppy—"

"That's enough sad talk for tonight." Mom puts on a big, fake smile. "Could you believe the assistant's name—Misty Woods? What a hoot! And that hair. What was she thinking?"

11

 y cell phone vibrates during study hall Friday morning. Of course, we're not supposed to have them turned on at school, and of course, everyone does. My heart skips. Mom's the only person with my number. Is it good news or bad?

Mrs. Russell is checking papers at her desk, so I slip to the back of the room and pretend to be looking at the books in the class library. She gives us required reading for English Lit every week, but who has time for that? I just fill out my log on Friday and Mom signs it—no questions asked.

"Hello." It's more a breath than a whisper, but I feel like everyone can hear me.

"We got a callback!" Mom screams into the phone, and I jerk it away from my ear. "One-thirty next Tuesday."

"Already?" My heart turns a somersault. The project's moving faster than either of us thought it would.

"We made it past the first hurdle! Aren't you thrilled, princess?"

"Over the moon and stars, Mom." I glance over my shoulder. Mrs. Russell's red pen is working overtime on our essays, but her head is cocked in my direction. "But I can't talk. I'm in study hall."

"Why don't I get you out of there so we can celebrate? I'll take you to lunch."

Any other day I'd parachute out the window to escape school. "I've got a monster science test this afternoon. Anyone who misses it—and hasn't been diagnosed with a terminal illness—has to make up the test at Saturday school." One more example of how high school is ruining my life.

"How awful!" I hear the disappointment in Mom's voice. "Then we'll have to wait until tomorrow night to celebrate."

Other kids complain about their parents pushing them to study, but Mom's priority is my career, not my grades. As long as I do well enough to keep the teachers from bothering her and I graduate from high school, that works for her. And it definitely works for me.

"Why not tonight?" Playing dumb is worth a shot.

"Philomena's party is tonight. Remember?"

"I've been trying not to." With my luck, Martin Storm will be on the guest list. With or without him, the evening is guaranteed to be a disaster. How can I endure two hours with Philomena and a horde of muscle-flexing jocks? I wonder if they'll entertain themselves by comparing the size of their arm muscles or seeing who can lift Ms. W's car the most times. If I'm lucky, they'll hold a hamburger-eating contest and see who can drink the most Mountain Dew without throwing up. Just thinking about it makes me shudder.

Mrs. Russell is out of her desk and heading my way. "Bye, Mom. I've got to go."

Who else did Martin Storm call back—the stunning blonde in the midnight blue dress, one of the pastel princesses, or a dozen other girls I didn't see?

I can't let that matter. From now until Tuesday I'll immerse myself in Razzi. I'll breathe her air, walk her walk, dream her dreams. I'll be more Razzi than any other actress could possibly be.

If I'm lucky, Razzi's better at science than I am.

Dance class is a massage for my aching brain. Now that I've mastered the new routine, I don't have to follow Ms. Summers. I just feel.

Even Gypsy's barbs wouldn't faze me this afternoon, but she wanders in wearing a goofy smile. I've seen her hanging on that guy Derrick at school, which means she's harassing him instead of me. If she's the best he can do, too bad for him.

The music begins and I fly.

I leap and kick. *Disappear, science test disaster.* I twirl and thrust my elbow. *Out of my way, pastel princesses.* My palms drive forward. *Leave my brain, doubts and worries.* I pull my fists tight against my chest. *Fill me up, spirit of Razzi.*

I whirl and twist and jab at everything that stands in my way. Then my insecurities are gone, and I'm dancing— light and free.

12

$\mathcal{I}$f high school is purgatory, then high school *parties* are hell! As if bombing this afternoon's science test wasn't enough to ruin my day, I get to spend my Friday night in the underworld.

Flashing red and blue lights make Philomena's guests look like they're wearing death masks. The music is pulverizing my eardrums. And the air is saturated with hormones, sweat, and onion dip.

I begged Mom to let me stay home and soak in a tub of bleach to remove the lingering traces of Martin Storm from last night's audition, but no luck. A party invitation from Ms. W is a command, not open for debate. But why does Ms. W want me here? These kids aren't actors or models.

The crowd is at least half guys, which surprises me.

Philomena isn't the type guys pay attention to. But maybe jocks of both sexes stick together. Not many people are paired up, but a couple in the corner has been making out ever since I got here. At least, I think they still are. Ever since I saw his hands go under her shirt, I've made it a point to face the other way.

The furniture has been pushed back and three couples are dancing, along with several groups of girls. A few of the girls are muscleheads like Philomena, but the rest appear to be a variety of shapes and sizes. Although it's hard to tell in this lighting, for most of them makeup doesn't seem to be a priority. But, wearing makeup or not, every girl—except me—is talking to or dancing with someone.

The guys are doing the same guy stuff I see at school—talking too loud, shoving each other, and gawking at the girls. A lanky guy with shoulder-length brown hair is balancing a cup on his forehead, and the people nearby are cheering him on. On the fringes of that group, an overfed football type keeps lifting up his sweatshirt to show his chest tattoo to anyone who wanders by.

I feel as if I've been dropped into the center of a three-ring circus.

There is not one fruit or vegetable in sight, and the soda isn't even diet. Yet everyone here is normal size. How can they eat corn chips, peanuts, and sour-cream dip without growing rear ends the size of the Saylorville Dam?

I've never been in Ms. W's basement before, and now I know why. It's Philomena's World of Sports.

Every surface is plastered with images of muscle-bound people sliding and jumping and lifting. I'm sure they have scars and bruises from head to toe. What is the point of lifting the monstrous bar full of weights in that poster and putting it down again? No point, none. Muscle tone is sexy; muscles the size of bowling balls are grotesque.

The basement has everything, even a bedroom and a kitchen. Philomena must spend a lot of time down here. If I didn't know she was Ms. W's daughter, I would never guess they're related.

Philomena seems to be having a good time. After she got over the shock of seeing me—inviting me was so not her idea—she led me to the snack table and bolted. Now she's working the room, drifting from one group to another. And—unlike me, Miss Invisibility—people are talking to her.

The good news is that Gypsy and her dancing bears aren't here. The bad news is that I don't know anyone except Philomena.

I feel kids staring at me, but when I look around, they all lock eyes with each other. What is the deal? Will making eye contact with me cause permanent blondness? I'm not freakishly tall or anorexic; I have the right amount of body parts; I'm wearing jeans and a sweater like everyone else.

I don't suppose it matters. If one of them came over to me, I wouldn't know what to say. Okay, I could kill thirty seconds griping about the science test. After that, there's the weather—always a fascinating topic. Then what? If I told them about my audition or modeling or even dance, they'd think I was bragging. I'm a good enough actress to pretend to listen to their jock talk, but I'd have nothing to contribute. In less than two minutes we'd both be looking for a way to escape.

How would it feel to be the popular girl everyone wants to be around? The girl who knows exactly what to say and do in any situation?

I'm holding court by the drinks table, and the crowd around me is cracking up over the joke I've just told. When they finally stop laughing, I say, "Okay, guys, it's somebody else's turn. I've been monopolizing the conversation all night."

"No, keep going," a medium-tall blond guy says. He's been at my side since I got here, and I plan to keep it that way. He's wearing horn-rimmed glasses, and he looks remarkably like a picture of Dad when he was in high school. "Your jokes are hilarious."

Gypsy pushes her way through the crowd to get closer. It's almost embarrassing the way she worships me. But she doesn't have many friends, so I let her hang around.

"Thank you." I smile modestly. "But doesn't anybody feel like dancing? I know I do."

"Yeah! Let's dance! Great idea!" my crowd of admirers shouts. "Show us the latest steps, Oribella!"

I shake my head, and my hair sends off golden sparks. Girls at school are always begging for my beauty secrets. Although I graciously share hair and makeup tips, I'm by far the most beautiful girl at Highland. "Not tonight," I say to a chorus of disappointed groans. "But Gypsy is a terrific dancer. Why not let her show her stuff?"

Gypsy blushes, and her eyes tear up with gratitude. Her first steps are hesitant, but when she gets warmed up, she looks pretty good. Not as good as I do, but . . .

"May I have this dance?" The handsome blond holds out his hand. I take it, and he sweeps me into a dance that leads us out into the cool night air—

"Hi." It's Derrick, Gypsy's new heartthrob. His black hair is slicked back, and he's wearing a dark green sweater that makes his physique look awesome. He stands with the easy slouch male models use on the runway. How did he get to the party without Gypsy hanging onto his pant leg? "You're the last person I'd expect to see here."

His confident smile tells me he's a guy who knows his way around girls—as if the way they mob him at school wasn't enough of a clue. But I don't remember the sexy sparkle in his eyes. Or his cute dimples. Or—

"Me, too. I'm not . . . this isn't . . ." My stomach has gone quivery, and my brain is sending nonsense to my mouth. "Ms. W invited me."

Derrick cocks his head to the side like he's studying a zoo exhibit.

"I mean Ms. Whitehaven. Philomena's mother." I wish I still had the paper cup of soda sludge Philomena gave me because I don't know what to do with my hands. I twist a lock of hair around my index finger like a ring.

"Phil-o-men-a?" Derrick smirks. "You call her that?

And her *mother* invited you. That's hilarious!" He hooks his thumbs into his jeans' pockets and rocks back on his heels.

The quivery blob in my stomach bumps against my insides. "Why is that funny?"

He gives me a wide-eyed look. "No reason. I've just never heard anybody use Phil's whole name."

"Oh." I'm sure he's making fun of me, but—since I know less about guys than I do about weightlifting—I can't think of a comeback.

Derrick looks me up and down with a lazy grin. "So, I hear you're a model. With your looks, I believe it." He moves into my personal space.

If he's going for seductive, it isn't working. The sparkle in his eyes has changed to a nasty glint. I try to edge away, but my back bumps into the wall. "I-I've done some modeling. Catalogs and stuff." A chill like icy mouse feet crawls up my neck.

"Lingerie, I hope." Derrick puts his hands on my shoulders. He leans toward me, so close I smell onion dip on his breath. "Maybe you'll give me a private show."

My hands press against Derrick's shoulders, but his onion-smelling mouth crashes into mine, grinding my lips against my teeth. His lips are slimy, and his tongue slides into my mouth like a slug. If there was anything in my stomach, I'd throw it up.

Like a trapped animal, I whirl back and forth to break his grip. He pulls his mouth away, but his hands are still clutching my arms.

"Get off me! Get off!" My foot connects with Derrick's ankle, but he's wearing boots.

Finally, I find the right angle to jam my elbow into his stomach, and he lets me go with a grunt. My hands are braced against his chest, and I shove him with all my strength.

He's off balance and staggers a little but doesn't fall. Too bad.

Derrick sneers at me and wipes his hand across his mouth. "Don't get your shorts in a twist, blondie. I just wanted to see what it was like. Not that great."

He turns away from me and bows to the room.

Everyone in the basement is staring and smirking. Then a guy begins to clap—one beat at a time. Now they're all clapping, faster and faster, until the basement echoes with mocking applause.

Tears burn my eyes like acid, but I will not cry. Not in front of them.

I throw my hair back and strut. My vision is blurred, but I find my way to the door and escape. The fall air feels like a cool towel on my burning face.

My feet fly up the steps and away from the house. It's not until I'm half a block away that I realize a ripped-out chunk of my hair is wrapped around my finger.

Down the block, I crouch in the shadows like a fugitive. Mom is working at Bonds and won't pick me up for twenty more minutes, but I'd pay rent to live behind these bushes before I'd walk back into that basement. The weather is mild, but my teeth are chattering.

Shortly after I fled from Slug Lips Derrick, Philomena—Phil, I should say—poked her head out of the basement and checked the street. She's probably afraid I'll tell Ms. W what happened and get her into trouble. No worries. I'll never tell anyone what happened in there.

I unwrap the hair string from my finger. It curls into a perfect corkscrew, too pretty to be alone. Poor curl. I should have ripped out slimy Derrick's hair, not my own. I tuck it into my sweater pocket.

I don't want to bore my brain cells by thinking about putrid Derrick, but I do. I've spit out his saliva and wiped my mouth fifty times, but I still feel his greasy lips. He kissed me just so everybody could watch and laugh. Why? They don't even know me.

At school I keep to myself. I don't write vicious notes or spread gossip. I haven't done a single thing to anybody at that party. Why do they hate me so much?

By Monday morning I'll be the school laughingstock.

And how will that be a change? Everybody already whispers and stares at me. Nobody talks to me except Gypsy and her horrible hags, and their only purpose is to taunt me.

Let them whisper and stare. They can hang from the ceiling by their toes and blow me kisses. Unlike them, my life has a direction.

When I hear a horn honk, I jump. It's Mom, and she's pulled our van right up to the basement door! She toots the horn again. What if Philomena pokes her head out and tells Mom I already left? That cannot happen.

In a half crouch, I scuttle along the building to the back of the van. Then I pop up on the passenger side and open the door.

Mom shrieks and grabs her chest like she's having a heart attack.

"Oribella! Where did you come from?"

Mom's stressed enough without the details of my evening. "I got too hot from dancing, so I took a walk down the block to cool off. I didn't mean to scare you."

"Dancing, huh?" Mom gives me a hopeful smile. "So you had a good time?"

"It's high school, Mom. How good can it be?"

When I close my eyes and lean against the headrest, Derrick's giant lips rush toward me. How hard will it be to keep my eyes open for the rest of my life?

13

On Monday I slide into American History two seconds before the tardy bell. I have one and a half endless days of school to suffer through until my callback tomorrow afternoon. Yes, I'll have to endure Martin Storm's pawing, but at least he can make my dreams come true.

If I survive today.

While Mr. Armstrong takes attendance, I hear Morgan—Gypsy's frizzy-haired henchwoman—blabbing to the world "—and then Derrick bowed. Everyone cracked up."

Who better to spread the word? Morgan could win a rumor-spreading championship in her sleep. Whispers and snorts gurgle around the room like sewer water.

Why Gypsy—who has beauty and talent—hangs out with a lowlife like Morgan is beyond my comprehension.

I open my history notebook and copy the assignment from the chalkboard. But my mind leaves on a different mission.

I am an industrial spy, stealing the formula for a lotion that will cure blemishes, wrinkles, and general ugliness. With my diamond-tipped nails, I cinch the belt of my chic tan trench coat and tilt my felt fedora at a rakish angle. Using the thumbprint I've cleverly drawn on a tissue with eyeliner, I trick the scanner and gain entry to the laboratory. Smiling with satisfaction, I pause inside the door to savor my success. I blink at the bright lights and starkly white walls, but I'm not concerned because my flawless skin looks lovely in any lighting. With the utmost care, I detach the flash drive from my earring, plug it into the computer, and download the secret formula. Although I clearly don't need the lotion for my own use, I pluck three bottles from the refrigerator as instructed by my superiors and stash them in the pocket of my trench. Mission accomplished.

As I'm striding purposefully to my silver Ferrari, Morgan darts from the rat-infested alley behind the laboratory. Her hair—now a hideous shade of blue—hangs in greasy clumps, her teeth have rotted down to brown stubs, and the pores on her nose are as black as pencil leads. I recoil in horror, shocked that—against all reason—Morgan looks more repulsive than ever. She seizes my arm with her scabby hands and begs for just one drop of lotion. But I toss my hair and laugh in her face, condemning her to a lifetime of looking like herself. Ah, sweet revenge.

As I pass between classes, I am completely absorbed in

the posters for next week's mixer, volleyball tryouts, and chess club. I memorize the six pillars of character and the bullet points under each one. If anyone gawks or sniggers at me, I do not notice. I am much too captivated by the posting of this month's lunch menu and the football schedule.

Today Spanish is a relief. Mr. Frontino has everyone chanting along with a language tape, which severely limits gossiping. After we mangle the Spanish tongue, we only have five minutes to do the worksheet, so everyone is engrossed in filling in those pesky little blanks.

When the bell rings, I slide my binder off the corner of my desk. The rings pop open, and papers scatter. What a shame! By the time I—oh so neatly and carefully—replace my materials in their proper order, everyone else has gone to lunch. I'd love to eat in here, but when Mr. Frontino comes back from the restroom, he'll shoo me out.

I'm a dog in a show ring. And everyone at Highland is waiting to see what I'll do next. I cannot face the cafeteria.

As I slip into the almost-deserted hallway, I trip over a giant push broom. Mrs. Tucker, the custodian, catches my arm. "You okay, dearie?" When I tell her yes, she leans her broom against the wall and mops her face with a red bandanna.

"If you don't hurry, you're going to go hungry." She's

tall and broad, with curly gray hair and thick glasses that make her eyes seem as big as ostrich eggs. "Skinny little thing like you can't afford to miss any meals."

I know she's not really concerned. It's just adult babble. But it hits me: she's the only person who's spoken to me all day. I feel like an alien—stared at and talked about, but too bizarre to fit in. Ever.

It's like every other day, but—my throat closes. My nose clogs. Tears spurt out of my eyes. It's stupid to be crying, because those people mean nothing to me. But sobs are punching me in the stomach and shaking my shoulders. They won't let me go.

"What's the matter?" Her ostrich-egg eyes are looking at me upside down. Even while I'm crying, I'm thinking Mrs. Tucker must be a contortionist to bend over that far. "Other kids giving you a hard time?"

I can't answer, and I'm shaking too hard to nod.

Mrs. Tucker takes my arm and steers me around the corner. She walks me past the No Students Allowed sign, sits me in her office, and closes the door. The smell of pine cleaner and dust penetrates my runny nose. Even the tissue she hands me smells of it.

Strange notes that aren't really music are coming from her computer. Everything's a blur until I dry my eyes. On Mrs. Tucker's computer screen, cartoon dogs are frolicking around, peeing on little cartoon trees, fire hydrants, and dogcatchers. All the time, they're barking to the tune "School days, school days."

I smile. I can think of a few people I'd like to see them pee on.

"Better?" Mrs. Tucker hands me a handful of tissues, and I blow my nose.

"Yes. Thanks." I toss a soggy tissue into the wastebasket by her desk.

"A good cry never hurt anybody." She crosses her arms over her chest. "I'm no counselor, but I know that much."

It wouldn't be possible to feel much more awkward. "I just—I couldn't face the cafeteria."

Mrs. Tucker clucks her tongue. "Like packs of wolves in there. When they're not tearing at their food, they're tearing at each other."

Even though we're in her office with the door closed, she looks over her shoulder, leans in, and whispers, "If I was a student looking for a quiet place to eat, I'd sit in the stairwell behind the boiler room. Nobody uses those stairs but me." She smiles. "As long as the student picks up her mess afterward, I don't mind one bit."

"Thank you, Mrs. Tucker." The stairwell sounds like heaven.

14

Tuesday afternoon's callback is as easy as punch. Ms. W tells me to wear the same outfit and hairstyle and to play Razzi just the way I did the first time. To me, it sounds boring, but she says Martin Storm wants to make sure I can be the same Razzi over and over again.

Blackie has recovered her voice and is yipping into her cell phone when Mom and I get there. This time, though, the waiting room is empty, and she sends us into the casting room right away.

"Bell! Good to see you again," Martin Storm bellows. "And Bell's mother! Hey, Ma Bell! Get it?" He grabs Mom's hand and pumps it like mad.

Mom's smile is tight, and I know her hand is drenched with nasty Martin Storm sweat. *Welcome to my world, Ma Bell.*

I say Razzi's lines, exactly like before. Then Martin Storm asks me to play her sweeter, then again with more attitude. Misty Woods hands me new lines, and I read those all three ways, too. All that time I've spent channeling Razzi has drawn us closer than identical twins. I can summon her like a genie from the well of my imagination.

Martin Storm is as transparent as a window, and I know instantly what he does and doesn't like. Now that I've figured him out, I become the person he wants to see, just like I've done with photographers and pageant judges my whole life.

"Good work, Bell," he says when I finish. "We'll let your agent know what we decide." He starts to stand up from his desk, then changes his mind. "I'll keep my hands off your hair today. It would be a crime to damage that gorgeous mane."

I laugh along with everyone else, mostly from relief at not being pawed. But under the laughter, a worm of fear gnaws in my stomach.

Another hunk of hair came out in my brush this morning.

15

I will not dwell on the hair issue. I'll just baby my hair like I did the last time a tiny piece fell out, and it will be fine. I'd like to ask Mom how much her hair usually sheds, but she'd ask why I wanted to know. She has enough to worry about already.

I cross my fingers that Whirlwind Productions will call today and tell me I've been chosen for Razzi. But Ms. W says there will be three or four callbacks for a picture this huge. It could be weeks before the studio decides.

I slip into my usual seat at the back of math class and wait for the guy who sits in front of me to arrive. He's the perfect defense against algebra—wide and tall, with shaggy sheepdog hair. From behind him I can't see Mrs.

McCollum or the baffling equations she scribbles on the overhead projector, and she can't see me.

Life would be a lot easier if I'd inherited Daddy's math genius DNA.

We had math homework last night, but I didn't lug the book home. I cannot afford to ruin my posture like the poor girls I see hunched under those obscenely heavy backpacks. And what use could a movie star possibly have for algebra?

Still, if I flunk a class, I'll have to take it again next year, so I do what has to be done. Mrs. McCollum has us check our own homework—red pens only—but what she can't see won't hurt me. When she writes the answers on the overhead, I'll peek around Gigantic Guy and copy them onto my paper—like always. Only today it will be the whole assignment instead of a few problems.

The bell is two seconds from ringing, so where's my camouflage? Today, when I haven't done a single problem of my homework, is not the day for him to be absent. I look around and find him two rows to my left making moon eyes at Morgan. Couldn't he wait until this weekend to fall in love?

Before I can regroup, a stubby, mop-haired female plops into his desk. This will not do. The top of her head barely reaches my chin.

Then I recognize the person under the chopped brown hair—Philomena. We haven't even made eye contact since the Party from Hell. I was hoping to keep it that way until a month after eternity.

Philomena either hasn't noticed me or is ignoring me like I'm ignoring her. But I see her homework is finished. Jocks aren't known for being good at math, but the paper looks okay from over her shoulder.

The first five minutes of class are for asking questions. Mrs. McCollum is surrounded by math nerds bugging her about who knows what. Philomena gets up to talk to one of her jock friends, leaving her homework on the corner of her desk for anybody to see.

My pencil is flying. Lucky for me, Philomena's writing is easy to read. I have no idea if her answers are right, but this is no time to be choosy. In a flash, I have the front side copied. A quick look around tells me nobody is watching. I stretch forward, flip the paper, and—

"Mrs. McCollum, Oribella is copying Phil's homework!" Morgan's voice, shrill as a fire alarm, screeches above the chatter.

I freeze with my arm stretched out, like a statue named "Guilt."

Philomena turns and snatches her paper from me, but she's too late. Mrs. McCollum is on the alert.

"Girls! Come up here, please, and bring your homework."

My face goes from icy to burning. What could Mrs. McCollum do if I crushed my paper into a tiny ball and swallowed it?

"You two are *so* busted!" a guy in the next row gloats. I suppose Mrs. McCollum would notice if I kicked him.

Everyone stares as I follow Philomena to the front of the room. I try to look innocent, but my ears are scorching. Mrs. McCollum holds out her hand for our papers.

It takes two seconds for her to see they're identical. "I'm surprised at you girls." She launches into a lecture about cheating, but it's lost on me. Just tear up my paper and let me sit down.

"—so in addition to getting a zero on your papers, you both have thirty minutes detention after school."

Detention! We're rehearsing for the dance recital this afternoon.

"But, Mrs. McCollum," Philomena is practically in tears, "I didn't cheat. Oribella copied my paper while I was talking to Destiny." The look she gives me fries my eyelashes.

"Is that what happened?" Mrs. McCollum turns to me. She has a blue smear on her cheek from the marker she writes with on the overhead.

I should confess. Philomena is Ms. W's daughter—and I cheated, not her. But I flash on her Hell Party. Maybe she dared Derrick to kiss me. Even if she didn't, she never apologized.

I shrug.

"What does that mean?" Mrs. McCollum glares at me from behind her wire-rimmed glasses.

My mouth is glued shut. I won't lie to get Philomena in trouble, but I'm not going to help her.

"Then I assume Philomena is telling the truth." Mrs. McCollum hands Philomena her paper and tosses mine in the trash. "Be here at two-forty-five, Oribella, and bring your math book."

The walk to my seat is endless. Nasty looks and snickers hit me like chunks of ice.

Philomena drops into her desk with her legs sideways, blocking the aisle. I have to look down to keep from tripping.

Her cheeks are blotchy. "Thanks for nothing." Spit sprays out of her mouth. When she pulls her feet back, her shoe cracks into my ankle.

As I sit down, I look at the clock. Five minutes down; six more hours to go. Correction—six and a half. Another endless day of school just got longer.

9 text Mom that I have to finish a math test after school
so she won't come into the building looking for me.
As long as I show up for detention, Mrs. McCollum won't
call her to report my cheating ways. I hope.

When I dash out after my thirty minutes of imprison-
ment, Mom has the engine running in the circle drive.
The look on her face says I may have to jump into a moving van. It's not *that* big a deal. Ms. Summers isn't going
to kick me out of the recital because I'm ten minutes late
for rehearsal. She wouldn't drop her lead dancer—or the
$150 a week Mom pays for my lessons.

The van is warm and full of Mom's spicy perfume. I'd
love to snuggle into the seat and shut my eyes for about
a million years. Instead, I prepare for a lecture. "Sorry,
Mom, I—"

"We got it!" Mom grabs my shoulders and spins me toward her. Her eyes glitter like a crazy woman's. "We . . . got . . . the . . . part!"

My brain stalls. Then I understand—the movie, Razzi. I got the part of Razzi!

I lunge toward Mom, and my legs bump into the console. Somehow I get my arms around her.

"We got it! We got it!" We squeal and bounce up and down together until the van is rocking.

"Ms. Whitehaven called me this afternoon." Mom can hardly catch her breath. "I couldn't wait to tell you. And then, today of all days, you're making up a test! I thought you'd never walk out of that building."

I shoo away a pinch of guilt about my lie. A math grade is nothing compared to this.

"Whirlwind Productions is faxing the contract to Ms. Whitehaven first thing tomorrow. We have an appointment to go over the contract—and sign it, of course—right after school."

Mom squishes my cheeks together so that my lips poke out. "So no staying after school tomorrow. Okay?"

"More than okay!" I am at the happiness bursting point. While we're shooting, I'm sure to have a tutor, which is like having no school at all. That makes the deal even sweeter.

My head is purring with wonderful thoughts when Mom drops me off at dance.

Luckily, Ms. Summers is rehearsing the little kids first.

The "Tinker Bells" are practicing their dance—which has two turns and three steps—but they're awful even though the recital is next Saturday. The daffodils keep crashing into each other, and the butterflies can't flap their wings at the same time. A few of the kids are crying, and the rest are giggling. It's a disaster.

Since Ms. Summers is busy trying not to yell, it's no problem to slip into the restroom and change into my costume.

I hate changing in the bathroom. The floor is cracked and grubby, and the room smells like somebody's having her period. But because of Mrs. McCollum's stupid detention, I didn't have time to go home. Good thing Mom brought my dance bag.

The music is winding down, but my hair isn't up yet. I'm babying it again, so I braid it gently. I love my hair—thick and silky with just the right amount of wave. But it doesn't feel the way my fingers remember. Is it thinner, more fragile? Or is it my imagination?

I push my fears away and coil the braid on top of my head. I use extra-long pins so it won't fall down while I'm rehearsing. Ms. Summers is under enough stress.

When I come out of the bathroom, the Tinker Bells are still in their flower and butterfly formation. But now Gypsy is standing in the middle of them. Ms. Summers cues up the music and they begin their routine.

I bite my lip to keep from laughing because Gypsy is going to get trampled. And for the first minute, I'm right. The little girls knock into her and each other just like before.

Then they don't.

Gypsy skips among them—turning a daffodil, lifting a butterfly's limp wings. The Tinker Bells twirl when they're supposed to, and they all slide in the same direction at almost the same time. And Gypsy—dressed in a flowered one-shoulder top and a black jazz skirt—is transforming a jumbled mess into an actual routine.

When the Tinker Bells finish their number, all of us who are standing around break into applause. Gypsy and the little girls do an extra curtsy. Then they jump on her, laughing and hugging—and probably trashing her costume. But she laughs and hugs right back.

Gypsy and I have a lot in common: we're pretty, we've danced together for years, we both took modeling lessons from Ms. W. We should be best friends. But Gypsy's hated me ever since she had to drop out of the Whitehaven Academy. And I haven't done anything to change her opinion.

While we're lining up for our first number, I say, "You looked good out there."

Gypsy's eyebrows draw together. "You mean, dancing the kiddy dance? I knew you'd take a shot at me about that."

I resist the urge to mention the zit on her chin. Trading insults with her makes things worse. "No, I'm serious. You were great with those little kids. They'd never listen to me."

Although Gypsy's forehead relaxes, her eyes are wary. "It helps to have five younger brothers and sisters."

"Five! That's insane! No wonder your parents couldn't afford Whitehaven!" When I realize what I've said, I gasp, stunned at my own bitchiness.

Gypsy's mouth drops. Then her jaw sets in an angry scowl, and she stalks away.

"Okay, girls, stop talking." Ms. Summers claps her hands. "Remember, we changed the combination to pivot step, ball change, then flick."

When the dance begins, the music's rhythm escapes me. Why did I blurt that out when Gypsy and I were *almost* getting along? Was I born socially clueless?

The music ends, and I turn to Gypsy as soon as I catch my breath. "I'm sorry. That came out wrong. I didn't mean it the way it sounded—"

"Of course not," she snarls. "Tell me, do you get a stiff neck from looking down on everyone?"

"Fine. Have it your way. I said I was sorry." *So much for my feeble attempt at friendship.* I grab a towel out of my bag to wipe my face.

"Oh, and Ori-fice, that's a lovely bald spot on the back of your head." Gypsy pokes my scalp with her index finger. "Is that the new beauty queen look?"

A bald spot on the back of my head. My gut says she's not making it up.

My chest pounds, black spots swarm in my eyes, and my mouth fills with the taste of metal. The edges of the room go dark, and the floor tilts. My legs fold under me.

Fingers dig into my upper arms, but I'm sliding to the floor. It's cool and gritty. With everything spinning, I feel safer here.

I'm breathing and breathing, but there's no air. My fingers are icy, and they tingle in an awful, scary way.

Why can't I breathe? Am I having a heart attack?

Somebody crushes a paper bag over my nose and mouth. They're suffocating me. I squirm, and more hands hold my arms to the floor.

"Breathe into the bag, Oribella. You're hyperventilating." Ms. Summers' voice is soothing. "Take slow, deep breaths. In . . . and . . . out. In . . . and . . . out. There you go. That's right."

I stop fighting and discover I can breathe again. The bag smells like peanut butter, but the black spots disappear. After a few more breaths I push the bag away.

Ms. Summers helps me sit up. "Better now?" Her calmness tells me I'm not the first dance student to pass out.

"Gypsy, give Oribella her water bottle."

Gypsy leans over and smacks the water bottle into my hand. I don't want to look at her, but I can't stop myself. Her lips are turned down with fake concern, but her eyes are as smug as a cat's.

She can't wait to tell the world my hair is falling out.

17

$\mathcal{I}$ shake off the blackness and throw all my energy into the rehearsal so Ms. Summers won't call Mom. But she doesn't let me leave until I promise to tell Mom what happened.

I put on my most innocent face and lie like crazy.

When Mom picks me up, she's still bubbling over. She insists on a celebration dinner at our favorite Italian restaurant. "And take your hair down, princess. I want everyone to see how beautiful you are."

In the shower, I run cool water through my hair and saturate it with a fistful of conditioner, but my wide-toothed comb comes out full of hair. Tremors of panic flash up and down my skin. I cannot pass out in the shower.

I lean against the wall and breathe in-and-out, in-and-out, but the black spots are dancing in my eyes, and the universe is spinning inside my head.

Make it stop. Make it stop.

It's a chant and a prayer, but I don't know who I'm praying to. I want to scream for Mom, to have her make everything better.

But I can't tell her because this horrible thing can't be happening. Not when everything is perfect and all our dreams are coming true. Tears drench my face, mixing with the water from the shower.

"Okay, movie star, you've had enough spa treatment for one day," Mom calls through the bathroom door. "I made us a seven-thirty reservation. I know it's a little late for a school night, but this is one night in a million."

Maybe the tears wash out some of my panic or maybe it's because Mom sounds so relaxed and happy, but I answer her in a nearly normal voice.

Every problem has a solution, Mom always says. Tomorrow during study hall I'll search every Web site for the way to make my hair stop shedding. Before anyone— especially Mom—finds out.

But tonight, Mom and I are going to celebrate my movie contract. And it's going to take every bit of acting talent I have to pull that off.

As soon as we get home after dinner, I lock myself in the bathroom and examine my scalp. By using two mirrors and twisting like a contortionist, I find seven bald spots. They're the size of dimes or smaller, perfectly round, pink, and shiny. Six are on top and the seventh—the one Gypsy poked—is high on the back.

I pull a plastic bag out from under my sink. In it is every piece of hair I've lost, except the one Martin Storm pulled out.

It's impossible to count the hair chunks since they're all mixed together, but I'm pretty sure there are more than seven. So either I miscounted—which doesn't seem likely—or the hair that Bev yanked out has already grown back in. And if that hair grew back, the other places will grow back, too. That should make me feel better, but it doesn't.

The next day I spend my study hall on the Internet. The first sites I google are selling baldness cures for old men. Then I find a site for a disease called alopecia with pictures that turn my stomach. It shows people—even kids— with ugly bald patches surrounded by tufts of scruffy hair. They look like survivors of nuclear fallout.

I cannot bring myself to read any more on that subject. My seven teeny patches don't look anything like that!

I surf more sites and find lots of strange stuff. People with a bizarre condition called trichotillomania pull their hair out by the roots. That is *so* not me. I'd give anything to shove mine back in.

Another site says hair loss can be caused by tumors, hormones, or—this is so disgusting—ringworm. When I read the words "fungus" and "pus-filled lesions," I am out of there.

Just when I'm about give up, I find a site for teens. Now I'm onto something. It says too much shampooing, blow-drying, and styling can cause hair loss. Stress and not eating right, too. I could be their poster girl!

I've been under *major* stress. I've been eating rabbit food to keep my weight just right for modeling and the Razzi auditions. And my poor hair gets washed, blow-dried, and styled three or four times a day. Of course it's protesting!

I almost float out of my chair with relief. If I relax, eat right, and treat my hair like it's spun glass, in no time it will be as thick as ever.

18

The next morning I get up half an hour early so my hair can air dry after I shampoo. Step one of Oribella's hair restoration plan. Two more clumps come out when I brush, but I refuse to freak. I can't expect miracles overnight. I anchor the sides of my hair up and back with combs to cover the thin spots. Then I check myself from every angle to make sure nothing shows.

At breakfast Mom is as happy as a four-year-old with a purseful of makeup. The corners of her eyes turn up—no shadows today—and her skin is glowing. While she sways around the kitchen singing off-key, my heart sits like a lump in my chest. But it would be selfish to worry her over something I can handle myself.

"Earth to Rhonda." I make my voice light and teasing. "It's your daughter calling."

Mom swoops and lands a bowl of cereal on the table. "Rhonda to movie star daughter. Speak to me."

I've thought and thought about a casual way to bring up the subject without making it a big deal, but I blurt it out. "I think I should start taking vitamins—and drinking protein shakes."

The dancing is over. "Why, princess? Aren't you feeling well?" She feels my forehead.

"It's not that. With the movie coming up"—the reality of how my life is about to change pours happiness over me—"I'm probably going to be too busy to eat the way I should."

"You're absolutely right, princess." Her fingers trail down my cheek, and I wonder if she's remembering when her skin was young and flawless. "I'll pick some up today."

"Super." Step two.

"And, um, maybe we should drag out those meditation tapes you bought last year. To, um, help control our stress." Step three.

"Meditation it is." Mom laughs. "Any other requests, Dr. Bettencourt?"

"Just take two aspirin and see me after school," I say in a gruff voice.

"*Right* after school. Because today we sign our first movie contract!" Mom pulls me out of my chair, and we polka around the room, giggling like kindergartners.

* * *

The day seems to last months and months, but it eventually ends. When Mom and I pull up to the Whitehaven Academy, my stomach is hopping like a frog in a jar.

Ms. W opens the door before Mom touches the handle. If I had any doubt today is extra, extra special, it's gone now.

"Rhonda, Oribella, please come in." Ms. W's smile is so wide her teeth show. "This is an exceptional day for you—and for the Whitehaven Agency."

Mom looks like a little kid getting a gold star. As far as I know, this is the only time Ms. W has called her by her first name.

As Ms. W escorts us to her office, I glance to make sure Philomena isn't lurking nearby. She's not. I'm sure she didn't tell Ms. W about the copying thing. I doubt they actually speak to each other.

Ms. W slides a stapled bundle of papers across her desk. "It's a pretty standard movie contract, but I was able to get you quite a generous arrangement, especially for your first role."

She smiles for the second time. The news must be awesome. "One thousand dollars a day *plus* living expenses. That means your transportation to and from the set and all meals will be covered during the filming. You will have your own trailer to use between takes. And—this took some negotiating—Oribella will keep her wardrobe. If the movie does well, you will be able to sell those items for a considerable sum."

Mom and I grin at each other. The money will more than make up for the time she'll miss at work. And when this movie leads to another, and another, she'll never have to work again.

"Tutoring will be provided on the set during filming— approximately six weeks—which is scheduled to begin just after the first of the year."

Tutoring, yes! And shooting doesn't begin for two and a half months, so I'll have plenty of time to get my hair healthy.

"Of course, there are the usual clauses about what signifies breach of contract: morals, failure to appear, health, and physical appearance are a few of those. Because Whirlwind Productions gears most of its movies toward young people, they're stricter about moral decency than other studios. Not that I expect that to be a problem for Oribella." Ms. W's eyes twinkle. "You can go over all of this at home and call me if you have any questions.

"However, we should go over the section about Oribella's hair, since that was one of the factors that led to her being selected." Ms. W taps a French-manicured talon on a paragraph. "I know you girls like to experiment, but Whirlwind Productions is quite specific about the condition of your hair."

Fear grabs the back of my neck.

Ms. W settles her reading glasses onto her nose. "You are not to change the color, length, or texture of your hair." She looks up from the contract. "That means not even a trim to remove split ends. When you arrive on the set, the stylist for the picture will do any necessary trimming or shaping."

Mom runs her hand down my hair. "They have nothing to worry about. We'll treat Oribella's hair as if it's made of pure gold. Right, princess?"

I nod, because my throat has closed.

"I'm certain you will." Ms. W hands Mom a pen and points out the places where we need to sign. When it's my turn, I tighten my muscles to keep my hand from trembling.

Mom and I are almost out the door when Ms. W stops us. "My goodness, how could I forget? Miles Crawford, the director, will be in town three weeks from tomorrow. Naturally, he is anxious to meet Oribella. At that time you'll have costume fittings and meet the hair and makeup staff." She seems ready to clap her hands with delight.

Please don't let me faint. In three weeks a movie studio stylist will be looking at my hair. And it won't stop with looking. She'll want to shampoo and brush and run her fingers over my scalp to make sure the studio is getting its money's worth.

"Princess, did you hear that?" Mom nudges me out of my daymare. "Think how exciting that will be!"

I try my best to smile. "Sure, Mom. That's just what I was thinking."

Sheets of blond hair fall around me, so thick and heavy that I can't see across the street. Hair piles on the ground in drifts. Long vines of hair twist around my ankles. I struggle, but the hair piles deeper and deeper—up to my waist, my chest, my neck. My mouth is filled with hair. I pull it out by the handful, but there's more and more, and it's choking me to death.

I wake up flailing against the sheets, soaked with sweat. While I was sleeping, my hair wrapped around my neck, and a long strand is draped across my mouth. With a gentle touch, I unwrap myself. My heart stops thudding when I realize the hair is still attached to my head.

Then I sit up and see the pile of hair on my pillow.

My breath stops. I feel like I walked into a room and discovered a dead body. It might as well be. It's the corpse of my future.

It's been ten days since I signed the contract with Whirlwind Productions, and nothing I've tried to save my hair has made one bit of difference. The vitamins upset my stomach and the protein drinks gag me. And if stress is causing my hair to fall out, how am I supposed to get unstressed?

I scrape the hair off my pillow and sneak into my bathroom. The bag under my sink is puffy now. If someone found it, what would they think it was? A fluffy stuffed kitten? A long-haired toy puppy?

Maybe they'd reach inside, expecting to find a cuddly animal. Instead they'd pull out Marie Antoinette's decapitated head with poofy blond hair and a bloody neck stump where the executioner grabbed her hair and lopped off her head in one stroke.

Except if he grabbed my hair, it would come off in his hand and I'd escape—bald and free. And my poor hair would be decapitated. Is it called decapitated if it's hair? Or is it dehairitated?

I jump into the shower and run the water as cold as I can stand it. The icy waterfall coats my skin with goose bumps, but it clears my head. This is a bigger problem than I can solve.

After I've towel-dried my hair, I study myself in the mirror. My wet hair, thin and sickly, sticks to my scalp.

The bald patches are deadly land mines waiting to explode, and I've run out of ways to keep Mom from noticing. I grip the edge of the sink to steady myself.

Mom raps on my bathroom door. "So, my sleeping beauty awakes at last." I hear a smile in her voice. "Guess what? A messenger just dropped off your script!"

There's a pause. Mom's waiting for me to open the door, squeal with joy, or, at least, answer her. But I can't. Because when I open this door, our lives will be ruined.

"Oribella? Is something wrong, princess?" Concern is already clouding her happiness.

I bite my lips and reach for the doorknob. A spark of static bites my finger, and I flinch. But I keep reaching, and the door is open.

I bury my face against Mom's shoulder. She's warm and solid, and her arms surround me. Her bathrobe is soft against my cheek. Her hair is damp and smells like lavender. She will make everything right.

"My God!" Mom pushes me away. "Oribella, your hair! My God, your hair!"

I empty my lungs in a whoosh that's part fear and part relief. Now she knows, too.

Mom spins me around and pushes me onto the toilet seat so hard that my hip bones feel bruised. Hair drops into my lap as she paws my scalp like a mother baboon.

Sobs gather in the bottom of my stomach and bubble up through my eyes, nose, and mouth. My shoulders heave. Tears pour down my cheeks onto my hair-covered lap. But Mom keeps pawing, like the hair and the girl crying under it aren't even connected.

She snatches my face between her palms. I expect her to comfort me, but she smashes my cheeks together and snaps my head up. Her eyes burn me like dry ice.

"What . . . have . . . you . . . done . . . to . . . your . . . hair?" Each word is a slap.

My smashed-together lips twitch with shock. *What have I done?* I swallow and gulp, trying to pull some words from my brain into my mouth.

Nothing comes out.

Mom must see how scared I am because she lets go of my face and squats in front of me. "Just tell me what you did, princess, and I'll figure out how to fix it."

My hands tingle, and the bathroom lights fade in and out.

Mom shoves my head between my knees. "Slow, deep breaths. Slow, deep breaths."

I concentrate on my toenail polish. The pale pink has chipped off my left second toe.

"Better?" When I can breathe again, Mom smoothes my hair back from my forehead and helps me sit up.

I glimpse myself in the mirror on the back of the door. My whipped hair and flopped-open mouth make me look like a crazy person.

"Now, what new hair product did your friends talk you into trying?" Mom makes her voice light, like it's big joke, but it's too late.

Friends? I shake my head because I still haven't found any words.

"Whatever you did, tell me. I'll take care of it."

Mom has mended torn dresses and broken heels, repaired smudged makeup and chipped nails, and lifted my spirit when I'm discouraged. But the feeling of dread in my stomach tells me this obstacle is too big even for her.

At last the words come. "That's the trouble, Mom. I didn't do anything at all."

20

When Mom hears that my hair's been falling out for weeks—and no weird new product caused it—she freaks even worse. She calls Dr. Andiano, who I've been going to for years. Mom's so hysterical that Dr. Andi agrees to see us, even though it's Saturday morning.

Since the office isn't officially open, Dr. Andi takes us into an exam room herself. She's old—maybe fifty. Her hair is streaked blond with an inch or so of dark gray roots, and it looks like she never combs it. I guess doctors don't have time for stuff like that.

"Hello, Oribella. Rhonda." Dr. Andi's smile makes me forget about her gray roots. Her brown eyes glow, and her face rounds into chubby Mrs. Santa cheeks. "What can I do for you today?"

Now that I'm going to find out what's really wrong, I want to go home. Icy sweat coats the goose pimples on my skin.

Mom only gets two words out before Dr. Andi holds up her hand. "Let's have Oribella describe her symptoms."

At first I stumble over my words, but Dr. Andi sits on a stool and listens as if she has all day. "When it started a couple months ago, only a little patch of hair fell out once in a while. But now it's falling faster and faster, and I have bald places everywhere." I have to stop and clear my throat. "At least ten of them."

Dr. Andi hands me a tissue, and I swipe my wet cheeks. She asks me if I've been feeling sick—I haven't; if I'm stressed out—who wouldn't be; what kind of food I eat— low calorie and tasteless. The whole time Dr. Andi nods and writes notes in my file.

She lays my file on the desk. "Why don't you show me these bare spots?"

My fingers have them memorized. I part my hair and show each one. Her cool fingertips explore them. "Which one is the most recent?"

I tap it, and she tugs the hair on the edge of the bald spot. When hairs come away in her fingers, Mom gasps.

Dr. Andi lays the hairs on a paper towel and scribbles more notes. "I want to run a few tests, but I can give you my preliminary diagnosis. I'll be pretty surprised if I'm wrong."

My jaw will shatter if I clench it any tighter.

Dr. Andi takes off her glasses. "Oribella, I believe you have a condition called alopecia areata."

The words sound foreign and deadly, but I recognize them from the Internet Web site where the people looked like radiation victims. My ears fill with static, like a TV when the cable goes out. "Am I dying?"

"Absolutely not." Dr. Andi's voice is stern. "You have a long, long, *long* healthy life ahead of you."

The static fades a little, and I choke back a sob of relief. But if I'm so healthy—

"Dr. Andiano, I don't understand. What's happening to Oribella's hair?" Mom rubs her hand over her forehead.

"Although the research isn't conclusive, we believe that with alopecia, a person's immune system gets confused and attacks his or her hair follicles. The attacked hair follicles become very small, and those hairs stop growing."

I touch a bare spot on my scalp. "I'm killing my own hair?" The idea creeps me out.

Dr. Andi smiles. "Your hair isn't dead, Oribella. That's one of the funny things about alopecia. The hair in those bare patches is there, perfectly healthy, waiting for the signal to grow again."

Mom looks as if she's just gotten a stay of execution. "Wonderful. How do we get the hair-growing signal started?"

Dr. Andi clears her throat. I feel bad news coming. "Alopecia is highly unpredictable. Oribella may start growing new hair tomorrow, or she may continue to lose hair for an unknown amount of time. There's no way to predict how much."

As if she's forecasting the weather. *"There's a chance of failing hair this weekend, but our Doppler radar isn't able to predict how much. Stay tuned for the latest updates."*

We're drowning in silence. Then Mom asks in a small voice, "But you can cure Oribella, can't you?"

Dr. Andi crosses her arms in front of her chest. "On Monday I'll make an appointment for you with a dermatologist who can discuss treatment options. But, you might as well know this going in—alopecia has no cure."

Tension pulses from Mom's rigid back up to the tight lines around her mouth. Her hands clutch the steering wheel, and her angry eyes are fixed on the street ahead. She stalked out of Dr. Andi's office in front of me, and she hasn't looked at me since.

My heart is hammering, and I'm a step away from panic. I feel like I'm trapped with an irate stranger. "Mom, I'm sorry. I should have—"

"Don't, Oribella!" she snaps. Her eyes don't even flicker toward me. "Not now."

She knows I didn't do anything to my hair; it's not fair for her to be so angry with me. "But it's not—"

"Not a word." Her voice is shaking with fury. "Or I might say something we'll both regret."

I bite the inside of my lower lip to keep from crying. I know Mom's angry because I didn't tell her sooner. But doesn't she understand that I was trying to handle this problem myself—to keep her from worrying? Instead, she acts like I've chosen to lose my hair and ruin both our lives.

When our van pulls into the garage, I jump out while the engine is running and dash into the house. I pause inside the door, waiting for her to come in and apologize.

For several minutes there's silence. Then I hear the engine gun. I open the door to the garage, but Mom has already backed out and is driving off down the street.

21

$\mathcal{I}$'m flopped on my back in the middle of my bed, staring at the pageant trophies on my shelves. The afternoon sun shines on them, and they look like they're made of pure gold. If I close my eyes, I can still hear the audience cheering when I took my victory walk at the Crowning Glory. I thought that was the beginning of everything wonderful.

Unless they have pageants for girls with rampant hair loss, I'll never win another crown. What would the promoters call them? For little kids, "Tots in Toupees." Teens could be "Wenches in Wigs" or "Girls without Curls."

The script for *Razzi's Tale* is on the floor where I threw it. When I auditioned for the part, I was Razzi. Now I'm nothing at all.

Mom didn't come home until just before noon with

salads from the deli down the street. We ate them across from each other at the kitchen table, but we might as well have been on opposite coasts. After she told me she'd brought lunch, Mom went mute again. And our picked-over meals went down the garbage disposal.

Now she's downstairs researching alopecia on her laptop. When Dr. Andi said it couldn't be cured, I thought Mom was going to keel over. Or I was.

I keep thinking Mom's going to come in, hug me, and tell me we'll get through this together, like always. Instead she acts like *her* hair is falling out and it's *my* fault. She's totally shutting me out.

Maybe Dr. Andi is wrong. Diseases get cured every day. And she's just a regular doctor, not a specialist.

I rest a fingertip on each bald spot, connecting the dots on my head. Each one is as smooth and slick as the tip of my nose. They feel weird, like little islands of scalp hiding in my hair.

If I lie here any longer, I'm going to go crazy. I scoot off my bed and begin my dance stretching routine. Whether I feel like it or not, the recital's tonight, and Ms. Summers expects my best. I rotate my neck and shoulders. My muscles groan. Then I grab the barre on my wall and do some pliés to warm up my legs. I wish I were dancing right now—throwing my body around the room until I collapse, too tired to think. Instead my brain beats itself against my skull, like a bird in a glass room.

I spend a solid hour arranging my hair to cover the bald

spots. A French braid works best, but even then I have to spread the hairs over each spot and glue them in place with globs of hair product. Then I shake my head every way possible to be sure nothing moves. By the time I finish, I could fly to Oz in a tornado and not a hair would be out of place.

Recitals are my favorite part of dance. The music cloaks me with enchantment and sends me soaring. With the spotlight highlighting me—and the audience watching—my body is liquid magic.

But tonight Gypsy eyes me with a knowing smirk that clutches my heart like a fist. Backstage I avoid her, afraid she'll make a comment in front of the other girls or—even worse—Ms. Summers. I'm more than Ms. Summers' star pupil. We've been together so long that she's almost like a second mom. I couldn't bear having to face her pity.

Luckily, I've practiced the routines so many times that my body has them memorized. So my arms and legs go through the motions, even though my heart and soul are paralyzed with fear.

The rest of the weekend is a bust, too. Mom puts on a good front at the recital, but when we're alone, she treats me like I'm a traitor. She barely talks to me, and when she does, her eyes are focused somewhere else. I know she's mad because I didn't tell her about my hair. Maybe she's right. If I'd been treated sooner, the problem might be fixed by now.

*   *   *

Monday afternoon Mom drives us to the dermatologist. The atmosphere in the van is bleak. I read everything I could find about alopecia during study hall, and I know what Mom knows—the news is going to be grim.

The waiting room has gold foil wallpaper and carpet so thick I almost sprain my ankle walking to the front desk. The receptionist hands us a health history form to fill out—eight pages long. We finish that chore and wait another hour before a nurse takes us to the exam room. She's medium size with brown hair and a forehead that's been lifted into *I Love Lucy* surprise. Her lips barely move when she reads through the form and asks all the same questions again.

We wait another hour—which seems twice as long as forever—until Dr. Fazio strolls in. He's short and wide with black hair slicked back like an infomercial con man, and he's got the kind of leathery tan that ruins your skin. Fantastic. I've got a dermatologist who broils himself like bacon.

He introduces himself, sits on a stool, and reads the form Mom and I filled out without saying one word to us. When he finishes reading, he gets up, grabs a magnifying glass, and inspects my head.

I try not to flinch, but his hands trolling around my scalp repulse me. Am I doomed to being mauled for the rest of my life? The doctor pats my bald spots, and the pokey hairs around them spring back. The next thing I know, he latches onto a tuft of hair and pulls. Even though he's not pulling the least bit hard, tears come to my eyes. When he lets go, at least a dozen hairs are between his fingers. He lays the hairs on a white paper towel and looks at them through the magnifying glass.

"This appears to be a typical case of Type One alopecia areata," Dr. Fazio recites into a tape player while he's scribbling in my chart. "The patient presents with numerous small, round bald patches on her scalp. The characteristic exclamation mark hairs are found on the margins of the bald areas." He stops to scratch his peeling nose. "Prescribed course of treatment will be corticosteroid injected locally into the hairless patches. Schedule recheck and probable retreatment in four weeks."

I understand most of what he says because I read the same thing on the Internet—including the part about the injections. But hearing a doctor say the actual words makes me want to jump off the table and run.

But how can I run away from my own body?

"Doctor Fazio, you've done your examination and talked into your little machine." Mom's voice crackles with frustration. "When are you going to tell me what's happening with my daughter?"

I try to send her a grateful look, but she's focused on him, not me.

The doctor blinks as if he's just realized Mom is here. The world's most clueless person could tell she's pissed.

"I was dictating my notes, Mrs."—he glances at my

chart—"Bettencourt. I have a large patient population, and I squeezed you in today as a favor to Dr. Andiano." He looks down his scaly nose at her. "I need to document my findings immediately so there is no confusion. You wouldn't want your daughter to receive the wrong treatment."

Mom blushes. "Of course not. But Oribella has recently signed a movie contract, and it stipulates that her hair be full and healthy." She crosses and uncrosses her legs. "So we have to reverse her hair loss right away."

"Then that's going to be a problem," Dr. Fazio says. "I can—and will—treat your daughter's alopecia as aggressively as possible. Although cortisone injections may stimulate regrowth in the bald areas in a month or so, it is quite likely she will continue to lose hair on other sections of her scalp."

My fingers bite into the table. How can Dr. Fathead be so rude and indifferent when every word out of his mouth is ruining my life? He's supposed to be helping me! I'd like to grab him by his greasy hair and smash his face onto the countertop.

An instant later, rage gives way to panic. Because if what he says is true, no matter what treatment I have, my hair will keep falling out. My beautiful golden hair, the thing I love best about myself.

This cannot be real.

Mom's face is white. "But we're meeting the director in ten days. There must be something—"

Dr. Fazio frowns. "The size and number of the hairless areas indicate that your daughter has been losing hair for some time now. If her situation is as urgent as you say, why didn't you seek treatment for her when the alopecia first presented itself?"

Mom cuts me a look, and my face feels like it's bursting into flames. "I-I didn't tell her," I stammer.

"I see." Dr. Fazio adds some more scribbles to my chart. "In most cases we would begin treatment with the injections only. Due to the *urgency* of Anabelle's situation"—he raises a bushy eyebrow—"we will treat her condition both topically and systemically. That way we're covering all our bases."

Topically and systemically. What does that mean?

"Will that work faster?" Mom's so eager to hear what he has to say that she doesn't correct him.

He gives her a superior smile. "With alopecia there are no guarantees.

"But after we complete today's treatment, my assistant can help you select a camouflaging agent. We have several creams and powders to minimize the appearance of the bald spots."

Dr. Fazio looks at his watch, which is as thin as my paper chart. It probably cost more than Mom makes in six months. "Now, as I said, I have a full patient load. If you're not ready to begin treatment today, you can schedule an appointment with my receptionist." He taps his pen on the counter.

"We're ready," Mom says without asking me. But she's right. There's no other choice.

Dr. Fazio pushes an intercom button. "Nurse, bring me three milliliters of a five milligram per milliliter solution of Kenalog. I'll need a half-inch, thirty-gauge needle."

Sweat is trickling down my sides, but my teeth are chattering, and a giant hand is crushing my lungs. *Don't be such a baby. It probably doesn't even hurt.*

When the nurse walks in with a tray of syringes and vials, my heart stops. I squeeze my eyes shut and bite the insides of my cheeks. I imagine Dad's voice, promising to take care of me, his comforting arm around my shoulders.

The doctor pinches my scalp and dabs it with something cold. My nose twitches from the bite of rubbing alcohol. *I think we read in biology that we don't have much feeling in our heads. Maybe that was the shot.*

A needle stabs my head, followed by a burning pain. My muscles go rigid. I bite the inside of my mouth so hard I taste blood. Tears squeeze from my eyes.

The needle stabs again and again, so many times I can't count them—don't want to count them. My head is on fire. I make myself breathe and will the pain to stop, but it goes on and on.

My eyes are watering, my nose is running, and I am hanging onto the table with both hands. The doctor has to know this is torture, but he keeps sticking me and sticking me.

I'm okay. I'm okay. The quicker he gives the shots, the sooner it's over.

My stomach is sloshing, but I will not get sick. *I'll picture the medicine rushing into my scalp, shaking my lazy hair awake, making it grow and grow.*

I'm not going to be sick, I'm not going to be sick, I'm . . .

The lights glow bright and dim, then they're gone.

22

When I open my eyes, I'm lying on the exam table with a damp cloth on my forehead. Nurse No-Name is checking my blood pressure.

Mom stands by my head, fanning me with a yellow folder. "You passed out, princess. Dr. Fazio says it happens sometimes."

It would be nice if someone mentioned that before we started. Then again, it was probably better not to know.

Dr. Fazio is gone. The nurse tells us he injected all of the bald spots, and today's treatment is over.

Hooray for that!

She shows us an array of creams and powders that are supposed to hide my bald spots. I let Mom look at them and choose. My head is throbbing, and throwing up still isn't out of the question.

Before we leave, the nurse gives Mom prescriptions for prednisone pills and a cream to rub on the bare patches. Pills and cream? Why couldn't we try those first? She also gives Mom a card with the date of my follow-up appointment in four weeks. My mouth goes dry. How can I go through this again?

The minute we get home, Mom says she's getting a migraine and goes up to her room. I suppose she expects me to take care of her like I always do—holding her hand, bringing her cool towels and ice water.

But when I was in pain, where was she? She didn't hold my hand or give me one word of sympathy when Dr. Vicious stuck my head a billion times. She didn't even hug me after I passed out from the pain. Is she so angry with me that she got some kind of perverse satisfaction from watching me suffer?

I know it's going to hurt, but I can't resist running my hand along my scalp—kind of like prodding a sore tooth. The top of my head feels like a lumpy potato, but it's not as sore as I thought it would be. That's something.

I grab a bottle of water and stretch out on the sofa. Now that my course of treatment has started, I have to generate positive energy, tap into my mind/body connection. Visualization techniques helped me with dance and becoming Razzi. Why wouldn't they work for growing hair? I set the water bottle on the floor and close my eyes.

With each breath, I form a mental picture of my hair follicles.

They're tucked into miniature cots lined up in row after row on my head. Their fair faces are shiny, and each little follicle wears a sleeping cap made of gold. Right now they're sleeping, and their tiny chests move up and down in perfect rhythm. I smile because they look so peaceful.

But it's morning and time for them to get up and growing. As the sun rises, a teeny bugler appears on the horizon of my scalp. Her long, yellow hair falls almost to her waist in glorious waves. When she lifts the bugle to her lips, I realize that I'm the teeny person. She plays a tune so rousing, a melody so compelling, that no follicle can resist its message.

With delighted smiles, the follicles spring from their beds and stand at attention. Their tiny feet send roots deep into my scalp, and a beautiful hair of pure gold sprouts from each one's shiny cap. In a matter of seconds, my scalp is covered with thick, glorious hair that grows longer and longer.

The phone rings me awake. I'd prefer to let the machine pick it up, but it might be Mom's job.

"Oh, hello, Oribella." My heart sinks when I hear Ms. W's gravelly voice. I'm not up to being perky right now. "Is Rhonda at home? I have some information about your meeting with Miles Crawford."

"I—uh—don't think I should disturb her, Ms. Whitehaven. She—uh—has a migraine." I can almost see Ms. W's frown through the phone. Whitehaven ladies never say "uh."

"Then I will trust you to take down the information accurately."

She waits while I fumble around for a pen and the notepad that's always by the phone—except for now. "Mr. Crawford will be flying into Des Moines on the Whirlwind Productions jet one week from Thursday at five o'clock. He has front row tickets to the Subterranean Flight concert at the Wells Fargo Arena, and he wants you and your mother to be his guests. The limousine will pick you up at seven o'clock sharp. After the concert, he has rented the dining room in an exclusive downtown restaurant for a private dinner."

Even I know Subterranean Flight is the hottest group going, but I'm too numb to be excited. One week from Thursday at seven o'clock my life will dissolve into a pile of goo. When the silence goes on too long, I manage to stammer, "Th-Th-That sounds exciting."

"Well, I hope you appreciate it." Ms. W is huffy at my lack of enthusiasm. "Miles Crawford is giving you the star treatment."

In a blur, I write down the information. How will Mom and I get away with this?

23

Mom's migraine is one of her worst. When I finally check on her, she has thrown up on herself, and her sheets are soaked with sweat. The smell of vomit gags me, but I sponge her off, change her sheets, and help her into clean pajamas. I shove the sheets into the washer. After she falls asleep, I drop into bed even though it's only seven o'clock.

The next morning I wash my hair gingerly. My scalp feels dented and bruised, like someone bounced it against a wall. And I don't own enough eye makeup to camouflage the no-sleep circles around my eyes. An electric current pulsed through my muscles all night, and my brain darted from thought to thought like a hummingbird on drugs. I can't remember ever feeling that wired, even the night

before my first audition. But I've never faced being bald—
or losing the biggest opportunity of my life.

"Good morning, princess. You look tired." Mom's face
is drawn, but she's smiling. "How is your head?"

Better, now that you're talking to me. "Not so bad. How's
yours?"

"Hurts like hell—just like I imagine yours does." Mom
grins. "But I'll live." She pulls a carton of orange juice
from the refrigerator. "Why don't I fix you some breakfast?"

"No thanks. My stomach is turning up its nose at food
this morning." After skipping dinner last night, I should be
starving, but the electric current is pulsing in my stomach
now, too. My heart feels quivery, as if it's beating so fast
it can't keep up. And there's a good chance the top of my
head is going to blow off like a Roman candle. It's probably nothing more than a colossal case of stress. Whatever
it is, I'm not going to say anything to Mom.

"You should eat something before school." Mom
frowns, and a line slices through the gap between her eyebrows. "I'll pack a little something extra in your lunch."
She pours coffee into a thermos for work. She loves Star-
bucks but hardly ever drinks it—one more sacrifice she's
made for me.

She opens the fridge and digs around inside. "When I
get home tonight, let's try those cover-up creams." I wonder if she's trying to make up for the way she treated me
yesterday. "Dr. Fazio's nurse said they do an excellent job

of concealing if properly applied. And, as I see from the note you left about Ms. Whitehaven's call, we have less than two weeks to learn."

How is blond-colored scalp cream going to fool anyone? But I tell her it's a good idea.

"I know those shots were brutal, princess, and Dr. Fazio was kind of a jerk—"

"Kind of?"

"Okay, a total jerk. But I read that many alopecia patients have had wonderful results from steroid injections, pills, and creams." Mom cradles my cheek in her hand. "I know you'll be one of them."

Tears sting my eyes. "I'm sorry I didn't tell you right away. I thought I could handle it myself."

"I'm sorry, too." Her hand drops from my face. "But what's done is done. We have to make the best of it and move on." She busies herself by washing a bunch of grapes.

My chest tightens. "It's not fair. Not now. I've trained my whole life; I've done everything right."

"Yes, you have, princess." She drops the grapes into a plastic baggie. "You've always been a hard worker. When you were still in diapers, photographers raved about your willingness to take direction."

It feels good for us to be talking again. I hate it when we fight. "I remember some of those shoots. They let me play with toys and puppies. And people made funny faces to make me laugh. I thought it was all a game."

"You didn't think it was a game in the fifth grade when you caught strep throat—"

"—and I couldn't be in the fashion show at the new mall. My heart was broken."

We look across the room at each other, each knowing what the other is thinking. That heartbreak was nothing compared to how we'll feel if I lose this role.

Mom folds over the top of my insulated lunch sack and holds it out to me. "But the next day you insisted on auditioning for Flip's preteen clothing line. We stood in the cold for hours."

I didn't tell Mom, but that day my throat was so sore and swollen I could barely lift my head off the pillow. "You didn't know it, but I got up at midnight the night before the audition and sneaked two extra antibiotic pills."

"Shame on you! I accused the pharmacy of shorting us."

"But I got to represent the whole spring line *and* keep all the clothes." I was so excited that I didn't sleep for a week. "So it was worth it." As I take the bag from her, our hands bump. Her skin is clammy.

"I suppose it was." She smiles a little. "And, when this ordeal is over and you see yourself on the big screen, those injections will be worth it, too."

She has to be right. The treatments will work, and my hair will grow in as thick as before.

Will a wish on a falling hair come true?

24

*M*om's hand sneaks over to tuck an imaginary strand of hair into my French braid, and I give her a *don't you dare* look. There is so much hair spray on my hair that an earthquake couldn't budge it.

I look as good as I'm going to. I just hope it's good enough to fool Miles Crawford.

Even if he doesn't see the yellow cover-up in the bald gaps on my scalp, will he miss the purple circles under my eyes? Or the bones sticking out everywhere from the six pounds I've lost?

After my out-of-control metabolism vibrated me through three nights of no sleep and three days of not being able to look at food, I finally told Mom something was wrong. When she called Dr. Sadistic's office, the nurse told her cortisone has "some possible side effects." After Mom read me the list the office e-mailed her, I was surprised to still be standing.

Even with Mom force-feeding me milk shakes, my revved-up body burned every calorie I swallowed—and then some. I've been shedding pounds faster than hair.

Still, today Mom has worked her hair, makeup, and wardrobe magic. My French braid looks thick and healthy, thanks to a hairpiece we found at a mall in Iowa City. We didn't dare shop in Des Moines where someone we know might see us. Mom braided it into my own hair so well I can't tell which is which. She used maximum coverage concealer to hide my no-sleep circles. If we stay away from bright lights, maybe we can pull this off.

When the doorbell rings, we both jump, but Mom recovers first. The crystals on her red velvet jacket sparkle as she strides to answer the door. Before she opens it, she turns and looks at me. "If you are confident, they will believe anything. Be magnificent, princess."

A chauffeur in a tuxedo stands at attention as Mom and I walk to the limousine. It's white and so long it takes up half the block. I can't see anything through the tinted windows. Snow drifts down like fairy dust, making me glad my skirt and matching jacket are lined.

Mom gets in first, and the warm smell of cinnamon and apples floats out. As I step in behind her, I lift my ankle-length, sapphire-blue skirt and see the twinkling crystals Mrs. Tran sewed around the hem.

"Good evening, Mrs. Bettencourt, I am Miles Crawford." A hand reaches out to shake Mom's, but all I can see is a shape in the shadows. Inside the limousine it's nice and dark. So far, so good.

"And you, of course, are my Razzi." Miles Crawford leans forward and spears me with his brooding eyes. He has a square chin, a wide mouth, and shaggy brown hair that tickles his collar. Knowing that he has the power to change my future makes my insides quivery.

He touches the dimple in my chin with one finger and turns my head from side to side. "Marty Storm has some qualities which do not bear mentioning, but he has excellent instincts and exquisite taste. You're perfect." His voice is as smooth as chocolate pudding.

A smile spreads from my toes to the top of my head. I sneak a thank-you glance at Mom, and she nods.

As the limousine pulls away from the curb, Miles Crawford reaches toward the bar. "Warm apple cider?" When Mom and I decline, he crosses his arms and leans back. "So, Oribella, I've read your creds, but I like to hear directly from my artists. What have you been doing for the past fifteen years?"

His eyes never leave me as I tell him about dancing and pageants, commercials and modeling. Mom tries to join the conversation, but Miles—he said to call him that—barely glances her way, and she gives up. He asks me question after question and listens to my answers like he's never heard anything more interesting.

At the concert, the celebrity treatment continues. We're whisked in through a back door and escorted to our private loge as the warm-up band leaves the stage. The loge has four seats—two in front and two in back. Mom steps down to the front row to let Miles and me sit side by side behind her. He motions for me to enter first. I hold my skirt off the floor and slide past him, fighting a sudden squeeze of claustrophobia. Which is ridiculous, since tonight is going perfectly.

But the pressure in my chest grows tighter and tighter. I perch on the edge of the padded seat, willing the feeling to pass.

Miles touches my arm. "Is something wrong with your seat?"

"Would it be okay if we switched places? In case I have to fix my makeup or something." I wince, knowing how juvenile I sound.

Miles grins. "Of course, Oribella. Whatever you wish."

After we change places—I avoid Mom's eyes—a waitress appears and asks for our drink orders. Miles orders a cocktail, but Mom and I both ask for water. My stomach is almost too jumpy to accept the cup of ice water the waitress brings me, but sipping it seems to help, and the closed-in feeling fades away.

I haven't been to a concert since I was seven and Mom took me to see Cinnamon and Roses, a girls' band I adored, as a Christmas present. The concert was held in the drafty old amphitheater across the street from here, and the only tickets Mom could afford were so far from the stage that the performers looked like moving dots and their voices sounded hollow.

This concert couldn't be more different. We're sitting in the lower part of the balcony with a clear view of the circular stage. Every seat in "the Well" is full—except the extra one in our loge—and a standing crowd packs the floor in front of the stage. The air hums with thousands of murmuring voices, and people roam the aisles, too energized to sit still.

Most of the audience is dressed in jeans and sweaters, and nobody I've seen is wearing anything nearly as dressy as Mom and I are. But Miles is wearing an expensively tailored charcoal gray suit and a light blue tie, so I don't feel too overdressed in comparison.

When Subterranean Flight takes the stage, the murmur of voices swells to a roar. Multicolored floodlights play over the crowd in an array of light and color that dazzles my eyes. Their first chord is so ear-shatteringly loud that I jump and cover my ears. Embarrassed, I glance to see if Miles noticed, but his focus is on the stage.

The four guys performing are model-thin, which is no surprise since they're constantly in motion. The two playing electric guitars bound from one side of the revolving stage to the other while the guy on the keyboard dances in place, his fingers flying across the keys. The drummer's arms flash from one percussion instrument to another, and the polished brass cymbals blaze with reflected light. While the crowd sways and claps, the auditorium pulsates with music so intense that it vibrates through my bones.

A giant screen suspended from the ceiling gives us close-up views of the performers. Their hair is short—not the usual shaggy rock-star look. Sweat pours down their cheeks, but they're hamming it up and grinning. Although I've never performed before a crowd this size, I can imagine the rush they're feeling as thousands of people shower them with adulation.

I recognize several of their numbers from hearing them on the radio, but I don't know the words well enough to sing along like the rest of the audience. Even so, I put my worries aside and allow myself to be swept up in the magic. Two hours later, when the concert ends after the second encore, my ears are still buzzing.

Afterward, Miles takes Mom and me backstage to meet "the Flight," as he calls them. The four guys—who look even thinner in person—are hanging out in their dressing room, toweling the sweat from their faces and chugging energy drinks from frost-covered bottles. Blotches of dampness mar their silky white shirts and black leather vests.

Mom catches my eye, and I know she's wondering if the stains will come out. But they're probably so rich they wear new outfits every night.

Miles introduces them, but their names slide through

my head like salad oil. Because I'm picturing myself in their place—surrounded by screaming fans, their adoration lifting me to unheard-of heights.

"Nice to meet you, Oribella," the lead singer says, shaking my hand. His face is flushed with heat and exertion, and his dark hair glistens with sweat. "Miles said you were gorgeous, but he should have said astoundingly gorgeous." He grins, looking younger than most of the seniors at Highland.

"Thank you." On the ride here Miles said we'd be going backstage, so during the concert I rehearsed what I'd say. "Your concert was amazing. I'm thrilled to have the chance to see you in person."

The short blond drummer steps in front of him. "Any time you want to see me in person, Oribella, just call." He hands me his card. "Any time at all." All of us laugh.

After a few more minutes of chitchat, we leave to finish our evening. Miles takes us to dinner at Splurge, one of the best restaurants in town. We're in our own private dining room where the lighting is muted and romantic.

Before we order, Mom and I excuse ourselves to the ladies' room. She dusts powder over my shiny face and makes sure my hair is still arranged just so. "He's thrilled with you, princess. It's a perfect evening."

Her voice trembles so slightly most people wouldn't notice. When she finishes powdering and I open my eyes, I'm looking right into hers.

I see cold, horrible fear.

"Ouch. I got some powder in my eyes." She makes a deal about patting her eyes and checking her makeup. When she looks at me again, she's all smiles. But her fear sticks to me like chewing gum.

"So, what did you think of the Flight?" Miles asks after we order. As he leans toward me, a lock of dark hair tumbles onto his forehead. He treats me as if I'm the center of the universe—the way Mom says Daddy did.

"I love their music." I could fall into Miles' eyes and never be heard from again. "And even though they're famous, they're so friendly, just like the guys I know at school." Which is almost the worst lie I've told tonight.

"Good." Miles pours more wine into his glass and takes a sip.

He pours some in a glass for me, too. If I take a big swallow, it might wash away the fear Mom planted in my stomach, but I won't. What if I got drunk and said something I shouldn't?

"They're performing the theme for *Razzi's Tale*." He looks at me over the rim of his glass. "To help promote the film, I've arranged for you to be in their next video."

A movie and a music video!

"That's wonderful." This is beyond a dream come true. "Thank you . . . Miles."

"No, thank you for being so charming. You're my perfect Razzi."

The rest of the evening Miles entertains us with stories about the famous people he's worked with. For a while I forget my fears and bask in being where I've wanted to be my whole life.

It's almost two in the morning when the limousine drops Mom and me at our front door, but I'm not the least bit tired. I'd stay awake forever to keep this magical night from ending.

"Thank you, Miles, for a wonderful evening," I say in my most grown-up voice, while my heart is singing, *I did it!* In three months, when I see him again, my hair will be thick and healthy.

"The pleasure was mine." He kisses the back of my hand. "But this is only the beginning. Tomorrow at the set you'll meet some of the cast and crew."

"Tomorrow?" Mom and I say together.

"You're quite a team." Miles chuckles. "I'll send the car around at ten o'clock to take Oribella to hair and wardrobe." He nods at Mom. "Of course, you're welcome, too, Rhonda."

He gives my hand a squeeze. "My only disappointment tonight was that you hid the magnificent hair Marty Storm raved about. Please wear it down tomorrow so I can see it, too."

25

$\mathcal{T}$he clock ticking on my nightstand reminds me of "The Tell-Tale Heart" from English Lit. Instead of a dead, thumping heart, I hear my clock saying, *Doom, doom, doom.*

I'm lying on top of my quilt, staring at the ceiling. Weak sunshine seeps through my sheer curtains, throwing dismal shadows against the wall. Although it's late afternoon, when I'd usually be at Ms. Summers' studio, for the past two weeks—my entire winter break from school—I haven't felt like dancing. Or walking. Or breathing.

And I never will again.

At least Christmas and New Year's are behind me. I know Great-Grandmother Eva's feelings were hurt when we canceled our plans to visit her, but she'd have a million questions about what happened to my movie role. And answering them would be like reliving that awful morning after the concert.

Since Mom and I already had the gifts under the tree, we went through the motions of exchanging them. I wish we hadn't. Even with Christmas carols playing on the radio, the mood in our living room was bleak. We undid the wrappings with too much care and said thank you as if we were strangers. And we were both too depressed to make Christmas dinner, so we ate turkey sandwiches and watched old movies on TV.

What was there to celebrate when everything we'd worked for was ruined?

Don't think about it. Don't. Don't. Don't.

But of course I do. I can't think about anything else.

The morning after the concert Mom thought we should tell the Whirlwind Productions driver I was sick, but stalling them another day or two wouldn't have made a difference. Waiting for the worst to happen was tearing my heart out piece by piece.

I brushed away the scarf she wanted me to wear, too. What was the point?

My naive little mind clung to the fantasy that Miles Crawford was too enchanted with me to settle for anyone else. I was his new protégé, the daughter he'd always wanted, the star he'd been waiting for. He'd look past my diseased head and insist on hair weaves, a wig, whatever it took to keep me in the movie. Only I could be his Razzi.

But the driver didn't take us to Miles Crawford; we went straight to hair and wardrobe. When the stylist ran a brush through my hair, his face turned white and he walked out. Mom and I stood, holding hands for an eternity in the freezing trailer, while I swallowed and swallowed to keep from throwing up. Ten minutes later the stylist walked back in, shook his head, and told us to go home.

Miles Crawford didn't fight for me. He didn't even care enough to leave his trailer. That afternoon one of his assistants called Ms. W. Then Ms. W called Mom and me, her voice so filled with fury I could hear her from across the room. By evening I'd lost my modeling career, my movie contract, and my agent.

The letter Mom and I received a few days later from Whirlwind Productions declared us in breach of contract. It said my alopecia was "a factor in the studio's decision," but my dishonesty "in attempting to conceal a disfiguring medical condition" was "unacceptable behavior from a Whirlwind Productions' employee. Those two factors combined leave us no option but to terminate Oribella Bettencourt's contract."

By then the worst had already happened. All the letter did was wriggle the knife deeper between my ribs. And drive the last wedge between Mom and me. Because every time she looks at me, I know she's thinking, *If you'd told me about your hair right away, would the treatments have worked in time?*

Since then I've been as invisible to her as a melted snowflake on the sidewalk. When she looks my way—which is almost never—her eyes go through me. When she talks to me—even less—it's about when dinner will be ready or something equally trivial.

Impossible as it seems, my appetite is coming back. I guess the side effects of the cortisone are wearing off. Too bad I haven't seen the good effects. Like hair. If anything, it's falling out faster than before. On Wednesday school starts again after winter break. I don't know how I'll face it.

I wonder if *Razzi's Tale* will begin filming on schedule. They could shoot around my character, but they've probably already replaced me with the streaked blond goddess.

Don't think about it. Don't. Don't. Don't.

"Please, I really need this!"

Mom's voice snaps my head off the pillow. At first I think she's calling me. Then I realize she's talking into her bedroom phone.

I creep into the hall to listen.

Her door's only slightly ajar, but I can hear and see her through the crack. A month ago I would have never spied on Mom. But a month ago I didn't need to. We were partners.

"Of course I know I quit last month, Claire. But your ad's still in the paper. The position hasn't been filled, has it?" Mom listens, tapping her foot on the carpet.

Claire—the manager at Butterfly Boutique.

"I'm sorry I missed so much work," Mom goes on, "but that part of my life is over. My daughter won't be modeling or doing pageants or"—her voice breaks—"acting any more.

"Please, Claire. Give me another chance. I really need the money. I'll work every Saturday and Sunday for the next six months." She pauses. "Yes, I'll put it in writing."

My heart sinks. More than half the modeling and commercial work is shot on weekends. If Mom's giving up all of hers, she doesn't believe I'm going to get better.

"This evening? That will be no problem. I'll be there in twenty minutes." Mom dabs her eyes with a tissue. "And, Claire, thank you. I won't let you down."

I barely have time to slip back into my room before she flies downstairs and out the door without saying a word.

The bills must really be piling up for Mom to beg Claire for her job back. Why wouldn't they be? There's no modeling or commercial money coming in. And all that money she was counting on from *Razzi's Tale* . . . Now there are doctor bills, too, and neither of Mom's jobs pays for health insurance. I wonder how far in debt we are.

Even though she's not here, I tiptoe into her bedroom. Her dresser shines with furniture polish, her perfume bottles are arranged in a neat, perfect design. Her drapes—the perfect shade of rose to match her carpet—hang open so they are exactly, perfectly the same on both sides of her streak-free windows.

Nothing in her room is marred. If something gets broken or flawed, she throws it away. No wonder she can't look at me anymore.

I'm looking for unpaid bills, so it takes me a minute to notice Grandmother Arianna's scrapbook on Mom's bed. When I was little, I pestered Mom to show me the scrapbook and tell me about my famous grandmother. But I stopped asking when I got old enough to realize Mom didn't like talking about her.

The early pictures are of Arianna as a child on her parents' farm. We look enough alike to be twins. Except Grandmother is never smiling, not even a little.

"She was almost too beautiful to be real," Mom said, "just like you, princess. More than anything, I wanted to be a glamorous actress like my mother. I begged her to come and get me, but she always had an excuse why she couldn't.

"Then, when I was sixteen, she died. And that ended that."

After Mom told me their story—hers and Arianna's—I'd lie in bed at night and think of Mom staring out the window, wishing her mother loved her enough to want to be with her.

Now I know how Mom felt.

I stretch out on Mom's bed and flip through the scrapbook. Nobody will say how Grandmother Arianna died, which makes me think it was something awful like suicide—or murder. If Grandmother Arianna had taken

Mom with her to Hollywood, would she still be alive? Maybe she'd have gotten her career on track and they'd both be famous actresses now. Of course, if Mom had grown up in California, she wouldn't have met Dad, which means I wouldn't be here.

My eyelids droop, and I rest my head on Mom's pillow. In a minute or two I'll get up and go back to my room.

"Oribella! What are you doing in here?"

Mom startles me awake. My eyes feel gummy. The green numbers on her clock radio tell me it's eleven-forty-five. Butterfly Boutique closes at nine o'clock. Is she just getting home?

Mom sways a little like she's crossing a rope bridge. Her eyes are ringed with mascara.

My mom, who never has more than one glass of wine, is drunk. "Mom, it's almost midnight. Where have you been?"

"Having a few drinks with my friends after work." She leans against her dresser. "I didn't know I needed your permission."

Her sarcasm stings me. "I didn't mean that, Mom. But I—"

"Everything's always about you—your pageants, your modeling. And, of course, your movie career. See how well that worked out!" Mom snorts.

Reality turns on its side. "What are you talking about?

You encouraged me to do all those things." I jump off her bed as if it's burst into flames. "*You* took me to modeling shoots before I could talk. You signed me up for baby pageants. You had me doing commercials when I was two."

"And you loved being the center of attention. Just like Arianna." Mom shakes her head.

Why is Mom bringing my grandmother into this? "I'm not like Arianna. She was—"

"I don't want to talk about her. She left me and never came back. But you were my second chance to be famous. Everyone would see my beautiful daughter and know that I could be perfect, too." Mom's eyes water. "Until you and your hair disease ruined everything."

Drunk or not, Mom's being unfair. She knows I can't control my alopecia. "It's *my* hair that's falling out, *my* life that's ruined. Not yours."

She keeps talking like she doesn't hear me. "I was so close." Her shoulders quake, and sooty mascara trails from the corners of her eyes. "You were supposed to be the perfect one. Why weren't you perfect?"

26

The next morning I braid what's left of my hair, wrap it on top of my head, and tuck in the ends. Even after I glop an ocean of gel on the sides and use a wide-toothed comb to spread hair over my bald spots, I see patches of scalp.

School will be awful today, but it can't be worse than being here. After what Mom said last night, I can't even call this home. I was awake most of the night, wondering how to get through the rest of my life without my career. Without my mom.

I dig around in my jewelry case and slip on the ring I got when I was crowned Primrose Princess four years ago. Today I need something to remind me I haven't always been a mutant. I sling my leather messenger bag over my shoulder and slouch downstairs to the kitchen.

When I pour myself a glass of orange juice, Mom looks into her coffee cup instead of at me. Her eyes are circled with red, and her skin is blotchy. I hope she's sick to her stomach and her head is splitting. I hope she feels so awful she wants to die.

Like I do.

As soon as I sit down, she gets up from the table and unloads the dishwasher. "We'll be working with the auditor at Bonds today, so I might be a few minutes late picking you up from dance class."

The orange juice burns my throat. I haven't been to dance for two weeks, and Mom hasn't even noticed. "I'm quitting dance. You can call Ms. Summers." How can I dance when my soul feels empty and my heart is broken beyond repair?

She jerks around and her lips tighten. Then she nods. "I'll let her know."

Mom knows how much dance means to me. I thought she'd try to talk me out of quitting. Tell me there's still hope. Tell me she loves me no matter what.

As I grab my bag and walk out, a piece of my heart dies.

During math class Morgan sharpens her pencil twenty times so she can slink past my desk and gawk at me. When she's not sharpening, she's whispering, passing notes, and pointing. Mrs. McCollum finally gets fed up and sends her to the hall for the rest of the period. It doesn't matter because Morgan's accomplished her mission—to make sure everyone notices I'm a hair-challenged freak.

When class ends, I see Morgan has put her hall time to good use, texting everyone she knows. Gypsy and her talking elephants have twined their trunks together by the water fountain. They make a big deal of not noticing me until I'm right across the hall from them. Then Gypsy swivels her head and lets out a shriek like she found a mouse in her panties.

Her gray-trunked friends turn on cue and stare. When they've made sure everyone in the hall is aware I'm the source of their terror, they clutch their notebooks to their perky breasts and stampede.

The spectacle is so bizarre I almost laugh. Everyone who hasn't bolted is watching to see what I'll do, so I throw my shoulders back and walk stiff-legged to the *T* at the end of the hall. For the rest of the morning, I stay out of sight as much as possible and slip into the back of each classroom just as the bell rings. But I'm a magnet for open-mouthed stares.

At lunchtime I duck into my private dining room. The stairway is stuffy but blissfully silent, and the stairs feel cool through my jeans. The dimness is soothing, but soon enough I'll have to face the stares again. Hello, rest of my life.

*   *   *

When everyone has gone into the cafeteria, I slip into the restroom and splash cold water on my face. I watch the water trickle into the chipped sink because if I see my reflection in the mirror, I'll smash it.

The bathroom door bangs open. Before I can duck into a stall, Gypsy and her swarm of skanks surround me. They reek of shiny new jeans and first-day-after-break girl musk.

Gypsy closes in on my left while the slut squad blocks me against the sink. She pokes her index finger into my shoulder. "What's wrong with your hair?"

The smell of boiled hot dogs on her breath gags me.

"If it's contagious, we have a *right* to know." Her screechy voice bounces off the walls.

Morgan, who is connected to Gypsy by an invisible umbilical cord, nods like a bobblehead doll.

Gypsy's eyes bug out, making her look like a psycho. "Morgan says you have hair cancer. If you do . . . that's not contagious, right?"

Morgan's head bobbles again.

"We're sorry for you and all that." Gypsy gives me another shot of wiener breath. "But if it's mange or head lice or a fungus . . ." She actually shudders. "Stay away from us."

Gypsy checks her girl gang for backup, and they all do the bobblehead thing. "So, are you contagious or not?"

You're an actress. Act.

Her gang is crowded behind her, trapping both of us. I

rub my palms—nice and slow—over my stiff, supergelled hair, coating my hands with major hair cooties. "I have alopecia areata, and it's *highly* contagious." My cootie-infested hands reach for Gypsy.

Her mouth rounds in fear, and the whites of her eyes flash all the way around her irises. She knocks girls aside like bowling pins and stumbles for the door.

"Stay away from me, you diseased freak!" Gypsy's minions let her pass, then stream after her like ants sucked into a vacuum cleaner.

Two seconds later I'm alone.

The bathroom is silent except for the blood pounding in my head.

News of this little incident will spread through school like a bad odor. Anyone who doesn't already hate me will think I'm diseased *and* insane.

A stall door creaks open. Philomena's messy brown hair pops out first, then her blocky face and square shoulders. "For a minute I thought I'd have to break up a girl fight."

I'm too surprised at seeing Phil to say anything.

"Who'd have thought Gypsy was that stupid?" Phil rolls her eyes. "She asked if you have *hair* cancer. Who's ever heard of that?"

"I guess Morgan has. She's the one spreading the word."

"Not surprising. If there's a rumor to be spread, Morgan's on top of it. Which—considering the size of her butt—explains all the squashed rumors at Highland High."

Phil grins, and a chuckle bubbles up from my chest. But before the chuckle reaches my mouth, distaste drops over Phil's face like a mask. She props her fists against her hips and looks me over.

"Your hair looks like crap." She sounds as impersonal as if she's telling me my shoe is untied. "No wonder Mom bailed out as your agent."

My face burns, but I refuse to take the bait. "She made a smart business move. Nobody's going to hire someone who looks like me."

Phil's eyebrows go up. "That's not why Mom—" She waves away the rest of her sentence. "It's not important now."

I turn and wash the hair gel off my hands. "Nothing is."

"Oh, please." Phil flicks her wrist like she's shooing a fly. "My hair is falling out. How can I live without being worshiped and adored?" She makes her voice whiny and obnoxious. "Boohoo for me."

Fury boils under my skin. "You don't have a clue what you're talking about."

"Because you're Oribella the Gorgeous, and I'm just a dumpy jock?" A vein stands out in Phil's forehead. Furious as I am, I notice that her hair is thick as a haystack. That is so not fair.

"I get it. You're glad my life sucks." I toss the paper towel in the trash and head for the door.

Phil crosses her arms over her chest. "What do you expect?"

"Look, I'm sorry I copied your math paper. I should have told Mrs. McCollum."

Phil groans and covers her eyes. "You think that's it? You are clueless!"

"Then what is it?" Where does she get off acting like *I'm* mentally challenged?

"*It is* that we've been in the same class since kindergarten, but you have never bothered to say one word to me." The vein in her forehead squirms like a snake. "And if for some reason you get trapped into talking to me, you act like you're doing me a favor."

My lips are stuck together. Anything I say will sound like a lie.

"You don't deny it. I guess that's something." Phil digs her fingers into her hair so that it looks more like a haystack than ever. "Just don't expect anyone to feel sorry for you—because they won't. The queen fell off her pedestal, and the peasants are cheering."

She catches the door as she walks out to keep it from slamming.

When I'm sure she's not coming back, I take off my Primrose Princess ring and flush it down the toilet.

27

"*I* wrote you a note to give the attendance office. It's on the table." As usual, Mom is standing at the counter with her back to me. Spooning sugar into her coffee must be such an exact science that she can't possibly turn around and face me. Although it's been three days since her little drinking binge, she hasn't bothered to apologize for the nasty things she said. "I'll pick you up for your appointment at one-fifteen."

I've had more than a month to prepare myself for this, but my stomach still jumps. "With Dr. Fazio?"

"Of course." Her spoon stops in midair. "He needs to see how well the treatment is working, and—"

"It isn't. Not at all." My non-hair is pulled back in a ratty ponytail. Not one hair has grown into the bald spots, new gaps are appearing daily, and the daily doses of prednisone along with my renewed appetite have made me as puffy as a water-soaked mushroom.

"Dr. Fazio will decide that." Mom concentrates on stirring the right amount of times. "I'm sure it takes more than one treatment to—"

"Okay, Okay!" I slam my notebook on the table so hard it pops open.

Mom whirls around. "I can't believe you're making such a fuss." She hasn't put on her makeup yet, and I notice the deep, tired lines in her forehead. "If I were in your shoes, I'd do everything possible to hold onto my career."

I shove papers helter-skelter into my notebook. "You never had a career, Mom, so how would you know?" It's a rude, nasty thing to say, but I'm in a rude, nasty mood.

My exit is flawless—scoop up notebook, toss nearly hairless head, storm out, and slam door without looking back. And I don't hate myself until I'm halfway down the block.

My early morning drama is wasted because I'm waiting for Mom outside school when she comes to get me for my appointment. Neither of us says a word when I climb into the van. All the way to the doctor's office we sit side by side, necks stiff, eyes forward.

When was the last time we laughed, or hugged each other?

The wooden-faced nurse leads us to an exam room. She asks a few questions, takes my blood pressure, frowns, and takes it again. Then she leaves, and Mom and I sit and wait.

Dr. Fazio's personality hasn't blossomed in the last month. He walks in, flips through my chart, then checks my scalp through a magnifying glass. "How often are you using the cream?"

He has to ask twice before I realize he's talking to me instead of his little recorder. "Once a day, like it says on the jar."

"Hmm." He pokes the little dents last month's shots left in my head. "You're taking the prednisone as directed?"

"Every day." And I have the squishy cheeks to prove it.

"Hmm." More poking, followed by the pulling out of my hair and examining it on the paper towel routine.

I'm surprised Mom isn't bombarding Dr. Fazio with questions, but she probably doesn't want to get scolded like last time. So neither of us says anything while he does whatever it is he's doing.

"This is a four-week recheck on fifteen-year-old Anabelle Bettencourt. No hair regrowth is observed in the bald areas, and continued hair loss is noted. Anabelle's blood pressure is . . ."

Dr. Fazio rattles on and on into his little recorder while Mom and I wait. But it sounds like Anabelle's treatments aren't working. Poor kid. I'm glad I'm not her.

Finally he pushes a button on his machine and looks at Mom. "So far the cortisone treatments haven't been effective. In addition, I'm concerned about your daughter's high blood pressure, which is probably caused by the oral prednisone."

"What do we do now?" Mom's purse straps are wrapped around her fist.

"Anabelle—"

"My name is Oribella, not Anabelle," I interrupt, mostly to remind him I'm not a piece of office equipment.

"Of course," Dr. Fazio huffs. "Stop taking the oral prednisone. Continue using the topical cream. And, as long as you're here, we'll do another round of injections." The usual chart scribbling. "Recheck in six weeks."

Mom's about to twist her purse straps in half. "But, Dr. Fazio, shouldn't Oribella's hair be growing in by now?"

He sighs. "As I'm sure I told you during your last visit, alopecia is unpredictable. And while we'd expect to see some regrowth after four and a half weeks, in some cases it can take as long as three months."

"So there's still hope?"

Dr. Fazio stops with his hand on the intercom button. "There wouldn't be any point in continuing treatment, would there?" He instructs his nurse to prepare the instruments of my torture. Then he says, in the sensitive way that I've grown to love, "Unless Anabelle is among the approximately twenty percent of my patients for whom there is no effective treatment."

On that positive note the door opens, and my favorite nurse walks in with a cloth-covered tray.

28

After seven weeks of staring and whispering at my falling hair, everyone at school is bored. I guess it's like watching puddles freeze—without the excitement. Even Gypsy and her ice-skating cockroaches sometimes forget to shriek and scurry when I walk past. Now that the drama is over, I spend too much time in my head. Not a good place to be.

It's bizarre, but school keeps me from dwelling on my wrecked life. Before my career ended, I sat in the back of class and tuned out the teachers' blah-blahing. The white noise made a great background for daydreaming. Now I sit in front, forcing myself to concentrate, to make sense of what they're saying. Not easy after all the school I've missed. But it's a great way to pass the time.

Each class is another forty-five minutes gone from my life.

The hours after school are an ordeal. I'm a plastic grocery sack caught on the wind—empty, tattered, going nowhere. At home, the silent phone haunts me. The pageant flyers in the mailbox burn my fingers like acid. And even when Mom is home—which is almost never—we're worse than strangers.

I have reached my limit. If I don't get out of this house, I'll go as crazy as Gypsy thinks I am.

My feet take me to the MTA bus stop. Yesterday's snow has been trampled into dark, shabby hills. The bus is crowded with middle schoolers headed to the mall. The girls giggle about who'll get the most valentines. The boys poke each other in the ribs. With a faux fur hat covering my head, I'm disguised as a normal girl. A guy about my age checks me out and smiles. If I whipped off my hat, he'd freak.

Ms. Summers' studio is only a few blocks off the bus route. I climb off the bus and head to the school. Class started half an hour ago, so the street out front is empty. Being here hurts like a toothache, but I'm pulled in with a force stronger than gravity.

As I slip in the side door, the familiar smell of warm bodies and Ms. Summers' signature perfume curls around me. The walls throb with music, and I ache to be caught in the rhythm.

My coat drops to the floor. The music is new to me,

but my body knows the moves. As I spin and leap, my hat frisbees against the wall. My head snaps—left right left—and my spindly ponytail slaps my cheeks. Air pumps into my lungs, clearing my head for the first time in forever. Dancing revives my groggy muscles, and they're hungry for more. How have I lived without this?

The music stops before I'm ready, and my energy drains away. Bags scrape across the floor as dancers dig for towels and water bottles. They're so close I can feel them breathing.

Like a thief, I grab my things and sneak out into the cold. The winter air creeps over my sweaty body, and I'm shivering before I get my coat on. Sweating after one number? I've gotten soft and out of shape.

For several minutes I stand on the sidewalk, listening to the faint swell of music as Ms. Summers' students practice the next number. But being this close without dancing is like picking the scab off a sore. So I turn around to walk back to the bus stop—and nearly crash into Phil as she's coming from the other direction.

"Cha-cha lesson finished already?" Phil is bundled to her ears in a navy-blue pea jacket. Her cheeks are shiny and red as frosted valentine cookies. And her hair is smashed under a pink and green stocking cap that dangles halfway down her back.

"I quit dance." I tug my hat down as far as it will go before I finish buttoning my coat.

"Burned out on it, huh?" Phil slaps her pink and green

mittens together. At least she's wearing something that matches.

I give her my best indifferent shrug, but my fingers tremble as I pull my gloves on.

"So what were you doing in there, spying?"

"Not spying." I clear my throat to hide the catch in my voice. "I'm spreading the hair cancer plague to innocent boys and girls."

"Fiendishly clever." Phil raises one eyebrow, and I have a crazy feeling she knows I can't face Ms. Summers' studio.

"Well, it's been real, but I'm freezing my butt off." Phil cups her hands and blows into them. "Good luck spreading your scourge." She gives me a little salute and heads down the sidewalk.

"Do you want to get a hot chocolate?" My voice cracks. The image of my empty house is strangling me. "You know, at a restaurant or something?"

Phil's eyebrow goes up again. She is as stunned as I am. But the invitation is hanging between us, and I can't take it back.

"Why not?" Her answer comes several beats too late. "Volleyball practice was canceled. I suppose I can kill some time and ride the activity bus back to school."

Phil waits for me to lead the way. But I have no idea where to buy hot chocolate in this neighborhood—or anywhere. It wasn't exactly on my modeling diet. And when Mom drove me to Ms. Summers' studio I was focused on my life, not the scenery.

She shakes her head at my cluelessness. "There's a coffee shop around the corner."

I turn the way she's pointing just as she takes a step, and we almost collide. Finally we figure out how to walk side by side without bumping.

My cheeks burn from the cold, but under my heavy coat I'm clammy with sweat. My breath roars in my ears. What was I thinking?

"What's an activity bus?" I say to break the silence.

Phil stops dead. "You aren't serious." When I nod, she rolls her eyes so high they show nothing but white. "Are you even *awake* during school?"

"Never mind. I was just trying to make conversation." Now I remember why I avoid Phil. She treats me like I'm an idiot.

"That in itself is a miracle." She opens the door to a shop wedged next to a hardware store and waves me inside. The warm spiciness brings back Mrs. Tran's dress shop. Suddenly I miss her so much that I drop into a booth to keep from falling.

"And we'll sit here." Phil doesn't bother to hide her sarcasm. She wads her coat in the corner of the bench and scoots in across from me.

My chin goes up. "Sorry. I just felt dizzy for a second. We can sit wherever you want."

Phil pulls off her hat and tosses it on top of her coat. Static electricity stands her hair on end. "Here is fine."

We order hot chocolate—Phil orders double whipped

cream; I order mine with skim milk—then we stare at the walls behind each other.

"The activity bus takes us to extracurriculars off campus." Phil taps the ends of her stubby fingers together. "Like today, the wrestling team is using the gym where we normally practice. Guys, of course, get top priority."

Our drinks come. She dips up a big spoonful of whipped cream and smacks her lips. "Mmm. You should have ordered this, Ori. You're missing out."

My drink tastes more like skim milk than chocolate, but the tiny sip I take makes me feel guilty. I wonder if I'll ever get used to being able to eat whatever I want.

"Anyway, the guys had the gym, so the volleyball team got shipped over to the YMCA for practice. On the activity bus." Phil emphasizes the last part. "Then Coach got sick at the last minute and canceled practice, but the bus had already left."

She drains her mug. Then she runs her finger around the inside to get every drop, pops her finger in her mouth, and slurps. *Gross.*

"So, our choices are the bus—either ours, which won't be back for two hours, or the MTA, catch a ride with somebody, or walk. Before I ran into you, I was planning to walk."

"But why? It's miles to Ms. W's—your house." I'm sure I've never walked more than five or six blocks in my life. Mom and I always had to be somewhere in a hurry.

"Exercise." Phil examines her cup to make sure no

chocolate was left behind. "When I miss a workout, I get grumpy and depressed. Don't you, now that you're not dancing?" She pulls a paper napkin from the table dispenser and wipes her fingers on it. Which I guess proves that a few of Ms. W's manners rubbed off.

I take another watery sip and push my mug away. "I'm depressed about a lot of things. It's hard to pick just one."

"Here we go again." Phil wads up the napkin and tosses it on the table. "Get off your skinny ass and do something for a change. You won't have time to be depressed."

There goes my theory about manners.

"What do you mean, 'for a change'? I've worked ever since I could walk. Now all that work was for nothing."

I cut Phil off before she can make another nasty comment. "If you injured your shoulder or your knee, and the doctor said you'd never play sports again, you'd be depressed."

Phil grunts, which I take for a yes—or at least a maybe.

"I'm not a jock, but I've trained as hard for my career as you have for sports."

Her expression says she doesn't believe me. Since I don't much care what she thinks, I keep talking.

"While you and the other kids were on the playground, I had to stay indoors. I didn't dare get a scrape or a mosquito bite because that could cost me a modeling job. When you were enjoying birthday cupcakes, I ate celery and danced an extra half hour to work it off."

Phil unfolds her wadded napkin and starts ripping it into pieces. I can't tell if she's even listening.

"I've taken dance since I was three years old—three or four lessons a week with hours of stretching and practice in-between. Try that and tell me it's not work."

Ignoring me, she arranges the napkin shreds in even rows on the table. Her jock arrogance is wearing on my nerves.

"In pageants I have to walk and sit and stand a certain way. If my smile shows too many teeth, I lose points." Phil looks up, and I bare my teeth. She rolls her eyes, but a smile sneaks onto the corners of her mouth.

"Modeling, acting, pageants—whatever—I have to follow directions exactly. Even then, whoever's in charge can wriggle a finger and I'm out. Just like that."

I'm out—just like that. I blot my eyes with my napkin. I am done crying.

"Okay, that's enough. You've convinced me." Her voice is gruff, but she looks almost sympathetic. "There's only one sure cure for depression."

She waves the waitress over and orders another chocolate. "You, too, Ori. A real one this time—not that low-fat crap. My treat."

What difference does it make? "Sure. Why not?"

29

"*A*re you sure you want to do this?" Phil is perched on the edge of my bathtub, tearing open the package of disposable razors I bought yesterday after our hot chocolate spree. "Maybe you should talk it over with your mom first."

"We've stopped talking." I run my finger along one blade of my shiny new scissors. Nice and sharp. "Besides, you're the one who said I look like an albino witch with radiation poisoning."

She grimaces. "That was a little harsh."

"Harsh, but true." I hand her the scissors and sit backward on the toilet. "I've stressed over this all day. Let's do it."

Phil lifts a strand of my hair. "Okay, here goes."

The scissors are cold against my scalp. I feel a pull as they slice through my hair.

"Uh, what should I do with this?" Phil holds up a clump of hair that looks like roadkill.

I've been preparing myself for this all day, but my stomach heaves and my mouth fills with acid. I grab the toilet tank and try not to think about what I'm doing.

"You just turned whiter than the bathtub. You're not going to puke, are you?" Phil presses a bottle into my hand. "Take a swig of my water."

I swish the water in my mouth and spit it into the sink. Three deep breaths. Another mouthful of water that I swallow. "There's a bag of hair under the sink," I manage to say.

In the dark behind my closed eyes I hear the cabinet door open. "Whoa! You've lost a lot of hair!"

"Thanks for the news flash." I keep my grip on the toilet tank. It's cool and slippery, but solid.

"Maybe you could—you know—get a wig made out of it."

I swallow and swallow. "Just cut it off. Okay?"

My eyes are glued shut as the scissors travel over my head. When the cold blades touch me, a chill runs up the back of my neck. But I've stopped feeling like I'm going to throw up.

"There. All cut." Phil sounds far away even though she's standing behind me. "You want to look?"

"I'll look after you're all done." Or in a couple of centuries. I resist the urge to rub my hand over what the scissors have left behind. "My shaving cream is in the tub."

"Just remember I've never done this before." Phil sounds worried.

"Really? I thought for sure you shaved two or three heads a week."

"Is that a jock joke?"

I open my eyes. "A what?"

"Come on." Phil waves the can of shaving cream around, and leftover tub water drips on my head. "Like all us girl athletes are so butch we shave our heads."

"First of all, since you have hair and I don't, that doesn't make sense. And, second, I'd be pretty stupid to make fun of you when you're getting ready to scrape a razor over my head."

"Good point. Here goes nothing." She squirts scented shaving cream over my almost-naked head, and the smell of cherries floods the room.

"My God! Is that ice water?" I hold back a shiver as freezing foam drips down my neck.

"No, Miss Picky." Phil grabs my jaw with one hand to keep me from moving. "Now hold still or you'll have a head full of cuts covered with toilet paper scraps."

I wince as Phil drags the razor from the front of my head to the back. "Hey, there's an idea," she says as she rinses the razor in the sink. "You could do commercials for toilet paper."

She cocks one hip and does the worst runway strut in

history. "Hey, girls, when I nick my head, nothing stops the bleeding like Fluffilicious."

In spite of myself, I smile. Shaving my head feels like cutting off my arm, but having Phil here makes it almost bearable. And, for the first time since I was diagnosed, I have control over something.

"Now who's making fun?"

"Okay, we're even on that one." She goes back to shaving, and I try to send my mind somewhere else. "But I still owe you for copying my math paper."

"And I still owe you for siccing Slug Lips Derrick on me at your party." What can I lose by saying it, except a chunk of my head?

Phil holds the razor under the water for a long time, and I wonder if she's deciding whether or not to slit my throat. "You can blame the ever-charming Derrick's presence on my cross-country teammates."

She hugs herself and bats her eyes. "You *have* to invite Derrick. He's sooooo hot!" Her lip curls. "If it was up to me, I wouldn't spit on him if he was on fire."

"Okay, that's why you invited Derrick. Why was I invited?"

"You were . . . Mom's idea. I told her you'd hate the party, but she felt sorry for you."

My jaw drops all the way to my collarbone.

"Keep jerking around like that, you're going to lose an ear." Phil slops more shaving cream on my head. "And you won't have hair to cover the stub."

"I'm pretty sure you can't cut my ear off with a Feather Touch razor. And there's no such thing as an ear stub."

Phil shrugs. "If you say so. But I'm an amateur at this. Anything can happen."

"What do you mean, Ms. W felt sorry for me?"

Phil shuffles around to my other side, and her Highland sweatshirt rubs against my cheek. It smells like fabric softener. "Mom says you never got to just be a kid and have fun."

I couldn't imagine Ms. W worrying about that. "Winning pageants was fun. Dancing, modeling, and acting were—"

"But don't you want friends? I've never seen you hanging out with anyone except your mom."

Mom was my only friend. And now the sight of me gives her a headache. Every morning I wake up hoping she's forgiven me and we can regain the closeness we had. But when she looks at me, her eyes are dull and angry, and I feel more alone than I ever thought possible. "Before . . . this . . . I was engrossed in my career. Now—"

"Now you're bald and beautiful." Phil plunks the razor into the sink and flutters her hands like a magician's assistant. "Behold! Ori, Queen of the Hairless Sophomores!"

A wounded animal moans behind us. I turn. Mom is framed in the doorway—her eyes stretched wide, her fingers spread across her horrified face.

30

$\mathcal{P}$hil's proclamation hangs in midair like skywriting. Her hands drop against her sides. "Uh, Mrs. Betten—"

"Please get out of here." Mom's voice is a groan, low and controlled. She steps back and points the way.

Phil pulls her jacket off the robe hook and walks out. Behind Mom's back she mouths, "Good luck."

Mom's face pales as her eyes sweep the bathroom, pausing at the bag of hair and the scum-filled sink. "Why?"

"Why not? Those ratty patches of hair looked like mange." I sound snottier than I mean to.

Each lock of hair Phil cut off severed a tie with my past life. My hair is history; my hopes and dreams are history. I have to accept that my career is behind me and somehow find a way to move on. No matter how hard it is, I'm not going to give up on life.

She closes her eyes for a couple of beats, and I know she's trying to compose herself. "I suppose you have a point," she says in the too-reasonable voice she uses with pageant officials. "This way, as your hair grows in, it will be all one length. So when you start modeling again—"

"Stop it!" My frustration and hurt boil out, and I wad up the towel and hurl it at the wall. "My career is over, Mother, because my hair is *not growing in*! The shots and creams and pills haven't grown *one single hair* on my head! And I have new bald spots everywhere!"

Mom's eyes close again, and she takes a deep breath. "I'm frustrated, too, but Dr. Fazio said it could take three months—"

"And then what—one or two hairs grow in while another five hundred fall out?" My knees are shaking. We're three feet apart in my dinky bathroom, but she won't look at me.

"So that's it?" The deep, composing breaths aren't working for her. "Instead of fighting for what you want, you're going to give up? Throw away everything we've worked for?"

What Mom said the night she'd been drinking still hurts. "You should be happy. Now you can enjoy your life instead of wasting time on me."

Mom runs a trembling hand over her hair. "When I was a little girl, I imagined my mother's glamorous life—the dresses, the parties, fans clamoring for her autograph—and I wanted to be like her. But then I'd look in the mirror and know I never could be." Her voice is low and dreamy as if she's talking to herself.

"Then you were born." Mom studies the plastic bag of hair on the floor. "And I realized I could give my daughter the chances I never had."

I'm here, Mom—a real, living person standing right in front of you.

"Since Lee died, I've devoted myself to your career. I knew you could reach the top. Mother didn't have the talent; I didn't have the looks. But you had both."

She sighs, and I hear the words she doesn't say. I'm the mistake, the ruined outfit she can't return. Her eyes shine with tears. "You were my dream come true. Perfect in every way."

I feel like I've been punched in the stomach. "Well, the joke's on you, Mother. I came with a no-return policy, and this"—I smack my smooth head—"is all that's left of your perfect princess."

I plow past her and fly downstairs, snatching my coat off the rack by the front door. I paw at the doorknob, the door crashes open, and I'm out.

The February air snatches at my naked head like an icy claw. I turn up my wool collar and hunch into it. It's not much help.

I turn right on the sidewalk and head down the street. I shuffle from block to block with my gloved hands over my ears. But my bare head feels like a penguin egg in Antarctica. The icy wind freezes the tears on my lashes until I blink, and the tear-icicles melt in frozen trails down my cheeks. I snuffle like a two-year-old.

Where am I going? I have no one to run to. No dad, no grandparents, not even a second cousin. Great-Grandmother Eva lives a hundred miles from here. I left without my cell phone, but so what? I don't have one single person to call. Phil is the only one who talks to me, and she doesn't like me. After tonight she'll never speak to me again.

When I can't stand the cold any longer, I head home.

My fingers are so stiff I can barely turn the doorknob. The house wraps me in warm arms that smell of cinnamon and vanilla—Mom's favorite potpourri. As I remove my coat, I see her sitting in her big flowered chair in the living room. A magazine is open in her lap, but she's staring at me.

I fling my coat at the rack inside the door and rush upstairs.

31

*B*eing bald puts me back in the center ring of the circus.

People stop in the hallway and stare with their mouths hanging open. Their hair is green or purple and gelled halfway to the moon. They've pierced everything but their big toes, and they're wearing Salvation Army rejects. But *I'm* the strange one.

Shoulders back, head up, one foot in front of the other. I can do the "I don't care" thing in my sleep.

In math I take my new usual seat in front. I can feel the eyeballs of everyone in class stuck to the back of my head like chewed bubble gum.

While I was brushing my teeth this morning, I finally got up the nerve to look at myself in the mirror—and encountered a creepy-looking stranger. My enormous bald head gleamed under the lights above my bathroom mirror, making my face look totally out of proportion. Overnight I'd turned into a freak of nature.

After I rinsed and spit, with my eyes closed, I made myself look again. No, I didn't look the same, but I was still *me*. My eyes, nose, and mouth hadn't changed a bit. My chin and cheekbones—and eyebrows—were the same. But my forehead had sneaked all the way to the back of my head. I struck a pose and giggled a little at how silly I looked.

Then I got out the hand mirror and studied myself from all angles. My scalp isn't as even as I thought; it's a landscape of gentle hills and valleys. I felt each one of them. Then I poured some lotion in my palm and rubbed it on the smooth skin. A few invisible nicks prickled, like after I've shaved my legs.

I took extra care with my makeup, adding an extra coat of mascara, a streak of eyeliner, and just the right amount of pearl-colored eye shadow on my brow bone. Then I feathered foundation from my face onto my scalp so I wouldn't look like I was wearing a skullcap. I applied blush with a light hand, and dug out my favorite earrings.

If nothing else, I'd be the best-looking bald girl Iowa has ever seen.

"I see you survived last night with no visible bruises." Phil says as she slides into the desk beside me. "Hey, no nicks, either. Excellent job, if I do say so."

I dig my homework out of my binder to hide my surprise. Since I copied her paper, Phil has been sitting on the opposite side of the room. "The frostbite must have burned them off."

She cocks her head to one side. "Say what?"

"I went for an unscheduled walk last night—bareheaded."

"Yeow! I bet you won't be doing that again anytime soon."

Mrs. McCollum threads her way through the class, handing out yesterday's geometry test. As she drops mine facedown on my desk, she whispers, "I need to see you after class."

I turn my test over. B minus. I check the name to make sure it's mine.

Phil gives my paper—and me—a sidelong look.

"I swear I didn't cheat!" But even I can't believe I got a grade this good. "Besides, I wasn't anywhere near you."

"You'd better be innocent, Ori." Phil shakes her head. "Only someone with a death wish would cheat right in front of McCollum's face."

After class I wait while a pushy girl with short black hair and glasses argues that the 98 percent she got on her test should be 100 percent. Spare me the drama.

Mrs. McCollum's lips are drawn tight, and I can imagine what she'd like to say. The poor girl finally shuffles off, forced to survive without an A plus.

As Mrs. McCollum turns toward me, my stomach feels

jumpy, which is totally unreal. Since when have I cared what a teacher thinks?

"Oribella, thank you for staying." She takes off her glasses and rubs the dents on the bridge of her nose. "I hope what I'm about to say won't embarrass you too much."

Embarrass me? After the last few weeks, that would be tough.

Mrs. McCollum smooths her hands down the front of her black wool jumper. "I'm aware of the—adversity— you've faced these past few months." Her eyes flick to my head. "Under the circumstances, I wouldn't have been surprised to see your grades and attendance suffer. But you've channeled your energy into becoming a better student—markedly better. I commend you for that." She smiles.

It takes a beat or two for me to get it, but she's praising me.

"You don't think I cheated on the test?"

"Sitting right under my nose? I *know* you didn't." Her smile widens. "Anyway, Oribella, I won't keep you from your next class." She picks up a handful of papers. "But it's gratifying to see you taking an interest in class. If there's anything I can do to help you—in any way—please let me know."

"Thank you, Mrs. McCollum. Th-that's really nice." The rush of pride I feel startles me. "Seriously."

32

I walk into the hall in a haze. A teacher applauded my brainpower. That's a first.

"Look, everyone. It's Ori-baldie, the world famous beauty queen!" Morgan shrieks. "I've got to have her autograph!"

She breaks out of the hag-pod and scurries toward me, waving a notepad in the air. Her purple mini hikes up over thunder thighs that shouldn't be seen or heard.

I walk on, determined to take the high road or at least the nearest detour. Then, bam! Morgan hits the floor with a jolt that rattles the test tubes in the science lab.

I turn to see Phil bent over, offering Morgan her hand. "Sorry, Morgue, but that was your bad. You cut in front of me." She hauls Morgan to her feet, and onlookers get a distressing view of Morgan's two-sizes-too-small leopard-print thong.

"If you don't watch yourself, next time you might get hurt." Phil's narrowed eyes are drilling holes into Morgan's face.

"Get off me, jockstrap!" Morgan pulls her hand free and almost falls on her rear again. "I'm going to—"

"Let it go, Morgan." Gypsy catches her upper arm and marches her away. "We've got class."

"Correction. You've got no class," Phil mutters at their backs. She walks off without a glance in my direction.

For the rest of the morning I try a new tactic. Whenever somebody stares, I flash them a big smile and say, "Hi! Your hair looks great!" The first few times my voice wobbles, but pretty soon I'm enjoying it.

Some people look at me like I'm mental, but by mid-morning girls I've never made eye contact with before are saying hi. Then I walk past a group of lean guys in swim-team jackets with heads as slick as mine. One of them calls, "Hey, gorgeous! I like your hair!" and we all laugh.

At lunchtime Mrs. Tucker sees me on my way to the stairwell. She props the dust mop under her arm like a crutch, studies me, and nods in approval. "Most females—including yours truly—would look like plucked chickens if they shaved their heads, but you look classy."

"Thank you" sounds weird, but I say it anyway. It doesn't seem possible, but I'm happier than I've been in weeks, happier than I've ever felt at school. I smile at Mrs.

Tucker and open the door to the stairwell, but a hand on my arm stops me.

"So that's where you go during lunch," Phil says. "And all this time I thought you were sneaking out to the parking lot for a smoke."

"I don't—" I sputter until I realize she's joking. "I don't smoke; I drink"—I think of something alcoholic—"margaritas with Mrs. Tucker."

"Don't drag me into this." Mrs. Tucker wags her finger at me. "It's high time you got out of that dusty stairwell and made some friends. Now scoot!"

Phil gives me a nudge. "You heard Mrs. Tucker. Time to show off your shiny new head. Let's hit the cafeteria."

My stomach lurches, but I go with Phil. The stairwell is dusty and depressing, and I'm tired of being an outcast. This morning people smiled at me, and I liked it.

But Derrick and his jock buddies are lurking just inside the cafeteria, and I know I can forget about being treated like a human being. Phil says hi to the guys and survives the gauntlet without a scratch to her ego. I don't expect to be that lucky.

I call up a smile and lock eyes with Jock #1, daring him not to smile back. He grins and runs his fingers through his hair. I can handle that. I tune the smile to dazzling and keep moving. More grins in return. Maybe I can do this after all.

"Ori-baldie. Ori-baldie." Derrick's jeering falsetto rises above the cafeteria clamor. "Look, everyone, Ori-bal—"

"Not cool." A guy the size of an SUV jabs Derrick in the ribs, knocking him sideways. "Treat the lady with respect." Derrick sputters, but apparently SUV Guy is nobody to mess with, despite the peace symbol shaved into his hair.

"Dwayne Overstreet at your service." SUV Guy sends me a gap-toothed smile. "Enjoy your lunch, Oribella."

"Please call me Ori." It's the first time I've used the nickname, and I like the way it feels in my mouth.

"Enjoy your lunch, Ori." Dwayne extends his arm toward the crowded room.

The cafeteria might be bearable after all.

Feeling encouraged but exposed, I follow Phil to a table near the center of the room. Five or six girls are already seated. Most are eating the school's interpretation of chef salad. A couple of them say hi to Phil, but the rest just wriggle their fingers because their mouths are full of food.

"Hey, team, this is Ori Bettencourt," Phil says, setting her tray in one of two open seats that are side by side. I take the other seat, grateful to be next to her. "Just so you know, I'm responsible for the striking new hairstyle she's sporting today."

"Good to know." The brown-haired girl across from Phil looks like she's trying to decide if Phil is serious. She has dark eyes and a full mouth that curves up at the corners. "Then I can sprint in the other direction if you come near me with scissors!"

The girl beside her studies me from under thick blond bangs that almost hide her hazel eyes. "No offense, Phil, but you might have cut it a little close this time." Except for her crooked bottom teeth, she's not bad looking.

Phil shakes her head. "Ori doesn't think so. Right, Ori?"

The other girls at the table have stopped eating and are leaning forward to hear what I say. But, unlike Gypsy and her Skank Squad, their expressions are curious rather than hostile.

I swallow, and I feel a blush creeping up my face. I wonder if my scalp is turning red, too. "Phil's right. This was my idea."

"All right, then." The towering African-American girl beside the blond nods her head, and her close-cropped black hair gleams under the florescent lights. "To each her own. If bald does it for you, it's fine with me." She grins, showing off perfect cheekbones and icy-white, even teeth. The camera would adore her.

"Thanks," I mumble, but they seem to be expecting me to say more. I don't feel like sharing the details of my alopecia with them. Maybe I should ask their names. Or fall back on my old standby—the weather.

Before the silence gets too awkward, Phil says, "By the way, this is the volleyball team—most of them anyway. That's Marietta," Phil points her fork at the brown-haired girl. "Serena's next to her and Shyasia is the one whose head is two inches short of hitting the overhead lights."

As Phil continues the introductions down the table, I nod and smile, but I'm so nervous that their names toss in my head like salad ingredients. After everyone has said hello, they pretty much ignore me to talk about their next volleyball game—or it might have been the last one they played. They're all talking at once, so it's hard to tell.

Since they seem to have forgotten about me, I'm free to watch and listen while they bat words back and forth— arguing, teasing, and laughing about almost anything. They all seem to know and like each other. Even though I'm sitting in the middle of their group, I'm an outsider. But, as far as I can tell, none of them hated me on sight, either.

Based on my school experiences, not being hated is as good as it gets.

33

After school I slump outside the chemistry lab while everyone else rushes to get on with their lives. The hall smells of after-gym sneakers and deodorant overpowered by I-tanked-on-that-pop-quiz sweat. The metal on metal of slamming lockers punctuates the general din. My scalp itches, and I stick my hands in my pockets to keep from scratching it.

Two of the volleyball players I sat with at lunch—Serena and Mari-something—smile in a halfhearted way when they pass. Like the rest of the girls at Phil's table, they were friendly, even though I was as out of place as an extra pinky toe.

After having people smile at me and laugh *with* me today, being bored and alone is worse than ever. They opened a teeny crack to a world I thought I didn't want, and I need to see more. Because the world I grew up in has shut its door in my face.

This morning I watched out my bedroom window as Mom picked up the newspaper from the middle of our yard. It was snowing, and I knew the paper would be soggy. I thought of all the times we joked about the paperboy's terrible aim. The places the paper landed were so bizarre that I bet Mom that someday he'd throw it on the roof. When we found it there one windy Saturday morning, she took me out for pancakes—a splurge for us. Most days Mom would spread the paper on the table and read me funny articles while I ate breakfast. Now she leaves for work before I come downstairs.

"Hey, Ori. What's up?" Phil says as she makes her way through the mob. "You look like a lost puppy."

"A Chihuahua, right? Aren't they the dogs with no hair?"

The hallway crowd keeps knocking into the beat-up gym bag slung over Phil's shoulder. "What is this, bumper cars?" she yells at nobody in particular. A guy with an Afro like black cotton candy grabs Phil's bag by the strap and spins her in a circle.

She shakes her fist at him. "Funny, Alfredo, just hilarious." He blows her a kiss and saunters off.

Phil drops the bag and kicks it to the wall. "I'm on my way to VB practice. The wrestling squad has the afternoon off, so we mere women are permitted to enter their sacred territory." She grimaces. "Enough about that. How was your first day as a bald goddess?"

"Better than I expected. Okay, actually."

"But . . ." Phil spins her hand in a *come on* motion.

"But, I miss"—*my life* "—being busy. I've got too much time on my hands."

Phil shrugs. "So join a club, take up yoga, learn Russian."

"Maybe I will, eventually, but it doesn't help me right now." Tears threaten to ambush me, and I banish them. Oribella was a crybaby. Ori laughs at disaster. Okay, laughing might be a stretch, but—

"Then come and watch volleyball practice." Phil retrieves her bag. "It's slightly less entertaining than watching snow melt, but it's a time killer."

I'm pathetically grateful for the offer. If she invited me to watch snow melt, I'd have done that, too. "You don't mind?"

"I can stand it if you can."

The gym is deserted except for a girl sitting in the first row of the bleachers with a pair of crutches on the seat beside her. I climb halfway up, take a seat, and jump up when my rear hits the cold metal. Is there a refrigeration unit under this thing? I fold my coat underneath my jeans and sit again. It's bulky, but at least I won't freeze to my seat.

The volleyball girls burst from the locker room, yelling and waving their arms like they're being chased by a serial killer. The empty gym magnifies the noise. If I call "hello" will it echo?

After the running around and yelling, the girls line up and slap the ball back and forth over the net. There doesn't seem to be a particular volleyball body type. Some of the girls, like Serena and Mari-whosit, are average size, but several of the players are taller than I am, and two of them—one being the African-American girl I met at lunch—look like redwoods. Phil is the shortest and stockiest of the group, but it doesn't slow her down.

I was supposed to play volleyball in gym last year, but I got hit in the head with the ball on the first day, and Mom got me a doctor's excuse until the unit was over. Black eyes and missing teeth are not photogenic.

When the girls are warmed up, the coach divides them into teams. She's wearing a gray sweatshirt with "Coach Boston" lettered on the back and baggy green shorts. Her hair is the color of cinnamon, and her skin is Caribbean-vacation brown. When she talks to the team, her voice is brisk, but she smiles a lot. The way she treats the players reminds me of Ms. Summers, and I feel a throb in the hollow place my dance lessons used to fill. Enough of that. Those thoughts are pointless.

I sort of know the rules for volleyball because last year's teacher made me write a report while the rest of the class was playing. Now, to keep from being bored, I try to figure out what's happening. To my surprise, I remember quite a bit.

When the game is over, one of the redwood girls goes over and talks to Coach Boston. The coach has to crane her neck to see Treetop's face. Whatever she's saying, Coach doesn't like it. Even from where I'm sitting I can see her frown. After Treetop says her piece, she heads for the locker room.

Uh-oh.

Coach tells the team to take a break and pulls Phil aside. They huddle, and the conversation looks serious. Then Phil looks up and points at me. Coach Boston looks up, too, and I feel a queasy ripple in my stomach. There is no way I should be the topic of their conversation.

When Phil calls me to come down, the ripple becomes a tidal wave. She can't be thinking . . .

As soon as I'm within earshot, Phil fast-talks like a telemarketer. "Hey, Ori. Jasmine had to pick up her grandmother at the airport, and that leaves us a player short. I told Coach you wouldn't mind filling in for our second practice game."

"You what?" Panic heats me from top to bottom. I must be glowing like a sparkler.

Phil grabs the shoulder of my sweater and yanks me down. "Come on, Ori. It's twenty minutes out of your life," she hisses in my ear. "You'll get some exercise, work off some tension." She jerks her head at the empty bleachers. "Nobody's watching."

Anxiety sticks my lips together, and they snap when

I speak. "My total volleyball experience adds up to ten seconds—eleven, tops."

Phil's not buying it. "All we need is a warm body. Rosie broke her ankle snowboarding last weekend." She glances at the girl in the bleachers. "Vanessa is out with mono, and Jessica's cold turned into bronchitis. They don't even qualify as walking wounded."

One of the girls calls, "Hey, Coach, I'm catching a chill. Are we going to play or what?"

Coach Boston waves, then turns to me. "Phil thought you might want to scrimmage with us. It's okay if you don't."

Phil's still holding onto my sweater. "Come on, Ori. Step up and take a risk."

My spine straightens at the challenge in Phil's eyes. "I would, but I'm not dressed—"

Phil pounces. "You can borrow one of my T-shirts. Jeans are a little stiff to play in, but doable. And sneakers are sneakers."

Before my head stops spinning, I'm wearing an extra-large T-shirt that's been moldering in Phil's gym bag for at least six weeks. The stench rolling off it burns the insides of my nostrils. As I take a place on the court, the girls on either side of me move away.

"Whitehaven, throw your gear in the laundry once in a while!" Serena yells at Phil from the row behind me. "Ori's going to pass out from the stink of that thing."

"She's not the only one." The tall black-haired girl on my right holds her nose. "That is not right."

Coach Boston blows her whistle. "Let's go, girls! We've only got the gym for forty more minutes."

Forty *minutes? Phil, you are such a liar.*

34

"Serving, zero-zero." Marietta, who—now that I know her whole name—is just called Mari, smashes the ball with her fist.

It sails over the net, right at me.

"Eeesh!" I squeak and cross my arms over my face. The ball bounces off me, and somebody taps it back across the net. Before I can breathe a sigh of relief, it's back in my space again.

Is there a target on my forehead?

I slap the ball away, hard, and the African-American girl leaps up like a ballerina and slams it to the floor on the other side of the net. A point for our side. How is that possible?

"Hey, nice assist!" She slaps my hand, which still stings

from hitting the ball. "We met at lunch, remember? I'm Shyasia, but call me Shy."

I barely choke out a hello before the ball is airborne again, served by my side. Since the ball seems determined to reposition my nose, my eyes are cemented to it. But staying out of the way isn't easy. When I duck away from the line of fire, the girls who are trying to hit the ball trample me.

After being bumped and elbowed a few times, I decide my only chance for survival is to hit the ball *away* from me. If it goes over the net, even better. Then I won't have my ribs crushed in a three-way collision when the girls around me dive for it.

I try to imagine the ball as Ms. Summers, and the rest of us as dancers. The Ms. Summers-ball leads the dance, and we follow. Sometimes we leap, sometimes we slide to the side, sometimes we spring back. The choreography is improvised, but it's still a dance.

When Coach Boston blows her whistle and announces the end of practice, I'm almost disappointed. Sweating and using my muscles again felt wonderful. I liked predicting where the ball would fly over the net—even though I was wrong half the time—and I *loved* knocking it back to the other side.

But done is done, so it's time to hit the locker room and ditch this rank T-shirt. Showering at school is too gross to consider, but I'll wash off the stink before I put my sweater back on. My poor bra may be beyond hope.

"Ori, got a sec?" Coach Boston stops me. She wrinkles her nose. "I swear I won't make you wear that rancid-smelling thing any longer than necessary."

"Hey!" Phil gives her a wounded look. "It's not that bad."

"It's worse." I wave the tail of the T-shirt under her nose. "I hope the odor hasn't soaked into my skin." An unfamiliar tingling tickles my scalp. I'd forgotten how much I enjoy teasing.

"Okay, you two. We'll have Ori fumigated later." Coach Boston sticks her hands in her pockets. Her smile reveals even, white teeth. "Ori, you're clearly an athlete. And you appear to have some natural talent for volleyball. Wouldn't you agree, Phil?"

Phil's eyes are darting from side to side. Is she surprised, horrified, or both? "She did okay—for a newbie."

"As Phil probably told you, we're down by several players." The coach doesn't seem to notice Phil's expression, which I'm 98 percent sure has settled into horrified. "I can't promise you much actual playing time, but you'd practice with the team and suit up for matches. And, with experience under your belt, there's always next year."

"You're asking me to join the sophomore volleyball team?" This is beyond unreal.

"Yes, I'm asking you to join the sophomore volleyball team." Coach nods her head with each word to make sure I understand. "We practice Monday, Tuesday, and Thursday. Matches are on Fridays—usually at the YMCA."

"Can I talk to Phil before I give you an answer?"

"Okay." Coach Boston draws out the last syllable until it's almost a question. "I'll be in my office for a half hour or so. Phil can show you."

As soon as Coach leaves, I say, "You hate the idea of me joining the team, don't you? Volleyball is your deal."

Phil rocks back on her heels and studies the climbing wall at the end of the gym. "I don't *hate* the idea, but I'm surprised you're considering it. Coach is desperate for players; that's why she asked you."

"Thanks. That's so sweet."

"You know what I mean." Phil wipes her forehead with the towel draped around her neck. "You could get involved in a hundred different activities. Are you sure volleyball is what you want? You're gonna get tired and sweaty—"

"Dancing made me tired and sweaty. I miss that." *So much that my chest aches.* I push the other things I miss out of my head.

"You'll get knocked around by the other girls, hit by the ball. Maybe in the face." Phil gives me a stern look. "Last season Shy's nose got broken."

I'm starting to get mad. "If you don't mind me being on the team, why are you trying so hard to talk me out of it?"

"When you join a team, it's not just about you any more. Your teammates count on you. Coach counts on you." Phil lets out a big sigh, like an impatient mother. "You're used to competing *against* other people, not working with them."

Now I've got her. "That's so not true. I've performed in dozens of dance recitals, and most of those dances were group numbers."

Phil grabs her hair in both hands like she's about to yank it out. "That's a perfect example of what I'm talking about. I've seen more of your dance recitals than I'd care to remember, and you are not a team player."

"You've done what?" Phil watching a dance recital is not a picture I can bring into focus.

"Mom dragged me to recitals for years. Most of her clients took dance, so she felt she had to make an appearance," Phil says. "And in each recital you were in the front row, oblivious to every other dancer on stage. If they'd all evaporated, you wouldn't have noticed."

I remember the music, the stage, the audience, the sheer joy of moving. But the other dancers? My mouth opens, but nothing comes out.

Because Phil is right. At every recital I was the star, and I expected the other performers to stay out of my way and let me have the spotlight. As long as I was satisfied with my performance that night, nothing else mattered. And if a number didn't go the way I thought it should, it was somebody else's fault. The other dancers weren't my equals; they were insignificant members of my supporting cast. When it came to being a team player, I didn't have a clue.

Suppose Gypsy doesn't hate me because I'm prettier or a better dancer or even because her family can't afford to send her to Whitehaven Academy? Maybe she hates me because I've been a self-absorbed, self-centered bitch. If I look too closely at the way I've acted, there's an excellent chance I'm not going to like myself, either.

"Like you said, volleyball is my deal. Sports are my deal." Phil's voice is dead serious. "If you're willing to make a commitment to the team, great. If you're not . . ."

Phil may not mean it as a dare, but it sounds like one to me.

35

Deciding I was going to be a team player was easy. Getting past fifteen years of spotlight hogging wasn't. During the first few practices I hung back, watching and learning. Then, as I became surer of my skills, I got caught up with wanting to be on center stage. Soon I was cutting in front of other players and robbing them of shots, even though they could have made those shots cleaner, stronger, and with more accuracy.

I'm surprised the team tolerated me. But they had their own way of putting me in my place. They knocked me on my rear, shoved me out of their space, and told me to pass the ball or die. Those tactics worked until the next scrimmage, when I got wrapped up in the competition and made the same mistakes all over again.

One afternoon, about two weeks after I joined the team, Shy took the seat beside me on the activity bus on the way to practice. The previous weekend she'd gotten braided hair extensions, and they were twined around her head like a crown. Despite her nickname, Shy is anything but and she didn't waste any time making her point. "Listen, Ori. Nobody's denying that you've got some raw skills. And who knows? Next year you might even get to start in a game or two."

When I began to thank her, she shook her head. "But that's a year and a whole lot of practices from now. Lately you've been pissing people off. You're busting into other players' positions, hogging the ball, and generally making a nuisance of yourself. You need to back off, girl, before somebody knocks your ass into the middle of next week."

I stammered out an "I'm sorry," but she waved it away. "No need for apologies. Just relax a little and have some trust that the rest of us know what we're doing. That's what being on a team is all about."

For a few practices after that, I was so afraid to get in someone else's way that I barely moved from my spot on the court. But Coach Boston and my teammates keep teaching me the ins and outs of the game, and I'm slowly learning to be part of a team. Most of the time I don't even mind the bumps and bruises.

* * *

But I will never, ever like lifting these stupid weights.

"They're barbells and dumbbells, not weight thingies," Phil says for the tenth time.

"I know, I know." Teasing her is great fun. "You add weights to the bar, so it's called a barbell," I recite like a good student. "And dumbbells are one solid piece. They're called that because anyone who lifts them is—"

"Watch your mouth, girl. With those spaghetti arms, you can't afford to piss me off." Phil has a fifteen-pound dumbbell in each hand, and she's lifting them out to the sides, but tilted forward. Like "pouring water from a pitcher," as she describes it.

I'm watching Phil in the mirrors on the wall of her workout room in Ms. W's basement and trying to do what she does. Except my dumbbells weigh two and a half pounds each, and my burning shoulder muscles are telling me to go home and take a long nap. "How is this going to improve my volleyball game? My arms will be so sore I won't be able to move them."

"You are such a wuss!" Phil puts the fifteens down and grabs the twelves. "My great-grandmother can bench press her own weight, and she's in her eighties."

"Now you're making things up." I drop my dumbbells on the rack and sigh with relief. Phil puts the twelves down and picks up the tens. She'll keep going "down the rack," as she calls it, until she's done fifty "reps" of shoulder raises. She's so strong it's scary.

While Phil sweats, I study her. All these years I

thought she was chubby, but she's all muscle. It's just that her clothes couldn't be less flattering. The gray sweatshirt she's wearing bags in all the wrong places, and it looks like the sleeves were hacked off in the garbage disposal. Her hair has no shape or volume. And I'm pretty sure she doesn't know cosmetics exist.

"So, what does your mom think of . . . all your sports?" I'm talking myself into a bad place, but I've been wondering forever. "I mean, all the different sports you play and the weight lifting and . . . well, it doesn't seem like you and Ms. W have much in common. Does she try to give you makeovers, or—"

"Has she totally given up on me?" I flinch, expecting Phil to bop me on the head, but her eyes are twinkling. "That is such an Oribella question. You think Mom and I aren't close because she works with actresses and models and I look like this?" She flexes her arm muscles and they bulge. *Really* bulge.

"But, you don't even live in the same part of the house."

"Come on, Ori. After you use a muscle, you've got to stretch it." Phil grabs her left elbow and pulls it across her chest toward her right shoulder. "That's a bad thing? Most of my friends would kill for this."

Good point.

When I try to copy Phil's movements, my shoulder muscles let me know they're not thrilled about being stretched.

"Besides, Mom is down here all the time."

"She is?" I can't picture Ms. W kicking back in jock town.

"How do you think she deals with all her spoiled brat clients?" When Phil sees the look on my face, she adds, "Not you. Seriously, Mom likes you, and she feels terrible about—" Phil clears her throat. "Anyway, she says you're 'remarkably unspoiled,' considering."

Before I can ask what "considering" means, Phil changes the subject. "Mom and I hang out together all the time. We love those old-fashioned board games— cribbage, Scrabble, backgammon—that stuff."

"You and Ms. W? But I thought—" Ms. W was only interested in beautiful people. That Phil was an embarrassment to her.

Phil sighs. "The more I'm around you, the more I understand what Mom means. You beautiful people are tiring."

"I'm not beau—"

Phil holds up her hand like a crossing guard. "Bald, tattooed, or in clown makeup, you're still gorgeous." She switches to her right elbow, and I do my best to follow. "Mom and I have had our problems. But we're lucky. So far we've been able to talk things out."

A feeling of loss sweeps through me. Whenever Mom and I talk, we make everything worse.

"And I'm working on Mom to live healthier," Phil goes on, oblivious to my mental state. "I've got her wearing the patch, and she's down to only two cigs a day. And . . . I talked her into cutting back on the Botox injections. She looked like a Muppet."

I swallow. "All this time I thought Ms. W ignored you."

"And because of that you felt superior to me. And now you're feeling sorry for yourself."

"I have a right." What does Phil know about it? "My career is gone."

Phil looks like she wants to shake me. "Nothing is gone except your hair and a part in an idiotic movie that nobody with a brain will go to see." She picks up another set of dumbbells—twenty-five pounds each—and presses them over her head. "Actresses and models wear wigs all the time. If a career is what you really want, there's nothing stopping you."

"Of course it's what I want. It's all I've ever wanted." So why do I sound like the computerized voice on our answering machine?

"Then go apologize to Mom and ask her to take you back as her client. She will, you know." Phil says it so matter-of-factly that I know it's true.

I'm numb with surprise. "After what I did to her?"

Phil sets her weights on the metal rack. She faces the mirror and shrugs her shoulders up and down. And, not knowing what else to do, I copy her. "When those people from the production company called to cancel your contract, Mom was royally pissed, probably the maddest I've ever seen her."

Our eyes meet in the mirror, and I cringe.

"But more than anything else, she was hurt and disappointed." Phil grabs two more dumbbells, hangs them at her sides, and goes back to shrugging. "Mom's represented you for fourteen years, give or take. You're more than just a client to her. She really cares about you. Her feelings were hurt that you didn't trust her enough to tell her what was going on."

As Phil's words soak in, I sink deeper in shame. To me, Ms. W was someone who existed to get me what I wanted. When my alopecia started, I didn't consider that misrepresenting myself to Whirlwind Productions would undermine her credibility as an agent. And feelings? Mine were the only ones that mattered.

"My God, Phil. I'm the most shallow, superficial, selfish person in the universe!"

"There you go again, Ori, thinking you're number one." Phil shakes her head, but she's smiling. "But I'm starting to think there may be hope for you yet. Now go knock on Mom's door, say you're sorry, and ask if you can please have your career back."

My arms wobble as I shrug the puny dumbbells up and down, but I've stopped counting the number of times because my heart is slamming against my ribs.

If my career meant so much to me, why didn't I fight to keep it? *Because when Mom stopped loving me, I gave up on myself.*

36

Ms. W's door is smooth, dark, and shiny as lip gloss, and I don't know if I can make myself knock on it. She'll probably turn up her nose when she sees me in a stinky sweat suit with no makeup, but I'll lose my nerve if I wait.

At least she won't say my hair is a mess.

My knuckles rap against the wood, which is as cool and satiny as it looks. And her voice, not as raspy as I remember, invites me in.

"Oribella!" Ms. W hurries around her desk. Her blouse is pale blue, her suit is the color of twilight, and her walk is looser, as if someone squirted oil on her joints. "How wonderful to see you!"

Then she does the most un-Ms. W thing I can imagine—

she hugs me. And it's been so long since anyone's comforted me that a sob jumps out of my throat. I hug her back, and before I remember that Ori doesn't cry, I'm bawling so hard that my back muscles feel like they're going to rip apart. She holds me tight, rocking and rocking me until my sobs become hiccups.

When I'm cried out, she hands me a wad of tissues and waits while I blow my nose. Then she leads me to an overstuffed suede love seat that's magically appeared against the wall where a stiff-backed chair used to be. I sink into the cushions and realize the magic is Ms. W. She's softer—her hair, her face, herself.

"Oh, my dear. You've been through a terrible ordeal, haven't you?"

I nod and snuffle.

Ms. W lays her arm across my shoulders. "I'm so sorry I haven't been there for you. I let my emotions, my disappointment and embarrassment, get the better of me. I—"

"No. It was my fault, every bit of it." I turn sideways so I can see her face and she can see mine. No more hiding. "The second my hair started falling out, I should have told you—and Mom. But I only thought about myself. I was scared, and I kept hoping . . ."

Ms. W squeezes my hand. "No further apologies necessary. That business is over and done with. We're going to focus on the future."

"I'm not sure what my future is." My voice breaks, but I bite my lip. Back to my "no crying" policy.

"Your future is without limits," Ms. W says in her no-nonsense voice. "If I had lent you my support instead of pouting like a spoiled child, alopecia would have been nothing more than a hiccup in your career."

She waves away my protests. "In the meantime, Phil tells me you've joined her volleyball team. Are you enjoying that?"

"It's . . . different, but yes, I am."

"Good, good, good. That's just what the doctor ordered." Ms. W claps her hands like a little girl. "And how is your mother?"

"Fine." Then I can't help adding, "I guess," in a way that says things between us aren't fine at all.

"I feared as much." I think Ms. W would like to say more, but a lady doesn't pry into other people's affairs. "This has been an upheaval for both of you. But you and Rhonda have a strong bond. Things will all come right in due time."

I nod, but my heart doesn't believe it. Ms. W and Phil may be able to work out their issues, but some things are too broken to fix.

She scoots back on the love seat and looks me over. "The shorn look is quite striking on you, Oribella. You're one of a very few women who could pull it off."

Like I had a choice. But I smile and thank her.

"However, you may want to purchase a wig for those occasions when you wish to . . ."

Not look like a freak of nature?

". . . have a less dramatic look," she says with a flourish. Her face is flushed from the search for a tactful way to phrase it.

She's being so nice that I pretend along with her. "Maybe someday. But synthetic wigs look tacky. And a human hair wig is out of our price range." *As if I'd ask Mom for the money.*

Ms. W grins from ear to ear. "Ah, but I have a solution. The Iowa Chapter of the Alopecia Foundation is searching for a spokesmodel—an attractive, confident young woman to appear in promotional advertising and to speak to other young people who . . . have the same diagnosis."

"A spokesmodel?" I'm getting used to being bald at school, but I can't imagine flaunting my baldness in front of strangers. "How did you hear about that?"

"My dear, I run a talent agency. When I read that they'd launched a fund-raising campaign, I contacted them to see if they needed someone."

I feel lower than low. Even after I made Ms. W look foolish, she went out of her way to find me a modeling gig.

"If you'd be willing to fill that role, you'd be fitted, through an organization called Locks of Love, for a human hair wig at no charge. They believe a young person like you can help girls—and boys—with alopecia to be aware of their options."

"I can be this spokesmodel if I want, no audition or anything?"

"When they see your portfolio and credentials, they'll snap you up. But, aside from the wig, there is no remuneration." Ms. W folds her hands neatly in her lap.

Which is a fancy way of saying I don't get paid. "Is it okay if I think about it?" Then I realize how that sounds. "It's not because they don't pay cash. But I've gotten kind of spoiled. If I don't feel like wearing makeup, I don't. If I want to eat a candy bar or drink hot chocolate with extra whipped cream, I do. I'm not excited about starving myself down to a size two again."

Ms. W takes both my hands. "The Alopecia Foundation doesn't want an anorexic waif. They want a beautiful, healthy girl like you." I look at her smooth skin and perfect French manicure, and my cheeks get hot. My cuticles are ragged, and I'm getting calluses on my palms from lifting weights.

"I'm delighted you're finally having fun, my dear. After all these years, you've earned the right to let your hair down."

Her eyes bug out, and I swear her own hair is standing on end. "I didn't just—How could I have said—"

We both burst out laughing.

37

I don't promise to be the spokesmodel, but Ms. W is sure she can still get me the wig. I'm not getting my hopes up because a free wig—even if it's human hair—will probably resemble a rat pelt.

This afternoon's volleyball game is at Highland instead of the YMCA. This is the second time I've worn my actual uniform, and it's fashion-lacking. The jersey is baggy, white, and sleeveless with Kelly green trim and numbers. The matching shorts—green with white trim—hang almost to my knees but still manage to bunch up in my crotch. Whoever designed the uniforms went for maximum ugliness with discomfort thrown in as a bonus. They should have hired Mrs. Tran.

Before the game, the locker room is filled with uncomfortable silence rather than the usual rah, rah team spirit. Coach Boston is on a rampage. Ceci, Sarah, and Jessica—who recovered from bronchitis a week ago—missed last night's practice. And Coach is a stickler that you have to practice to play.

"Okay, listen up." She's wearing her deadly serious coach face. "This afternoon's starters are Shy, Phil, Mari, Serena, Destiny, and Ori."

Gasps bounce off the lockers, and I'm stunned beyond words. Destiny has never started, but, unlike me, she's played in an actual game. My experience ends with scrimmaging.

Coach Boston ignores the looks of shock. "We're not going to let Roosevelt's five to one record intimidate us."

Hard to do, since ours is 1–5.

The pep talk goes on, but it's lost on me. What if I forget everything I've learned in practice? The girls have started treating me like a member of the team. They'll be mad enough that Coach gave me someone's starting position. If I blow the game, they'll hate me.

Halfway through Coach's speech, Phil is standing beside me. "No worries, Ori," she whispers. "Just be a team player. We'll have your back. You have ours."

Hearing that, knowing that, I'm lifted up. It's not all on me.

During the first game I cause two violations by touching the net when I'm trying to block. The pitifully few hits I make go straight up, but Shy and Mari tap them to the other side and save me from looking like a complete klutz. We lose 15–8, but we are all out of sync because our starters are sitting on the bench and Destiny and I are messing up everyone's rhythm.

By the second game my nerves are settling. Now that I'm not shaking, I have more control of the ball. If I keep it in play, one of the experienced players can score off my assist. Although Phil is short, she puts her muscles to good use. Her powerful serves crash like missiles into the Roosevelt players. And, just like that, we've won the second game.

Shy and Serena catch fire during the third game. It ends with a score of 16–14, and we've—miraculously—won the match. I'm giddy with relief. I didn't play that well, but I didn't blow it for us. I even had a miraculous dig when the ball was about an inch from the floor.

"Good game, Ori." Shy slaps me on the back, and my wet jersey sticks to my skin. *Ick.*

"Thanks." She congratulates everyone, but the praise still feels good. "You're amazing. You spike like a pro."

"Hey, you're on the way, girl. Just give it time." With her sculpted cheekbones glistening with sweat, Shy looks like a goddess. "You made some great assists. Right, Ms. Team Captain?"

"You said that." Phil grins wide enough to strain a cheek muscle.

I'm glowing inside and out. "Thanks. Somebody told me it's important to be a team player."

While we're changing clothes, Phil announces that we should all go out for pizza to celebrate our victory. Destiny has to go home and babysit her little brother so her parents can go out to dinner for their anniversary, but the rest of the starters are up for it. Phil also invites the girls who had to sit out of the match because they missed practice, but they beg off. I hope I haven't made more enemies.

While the other girls are blow-drying their hair, I step out of the locker room to call Mom. She's rarely home these days, but I can leave a message on the machine so she'll know where I am if she gets home before I do. It probably doesn't matter to her if I leave a message or not, but habits are hard to break.

The phone rings, and I wait for the machine to kick in, but Mom answers instead. "Oh, you're home." I have to stop and swallow, which is stupid. Who gets nervous talking to her own mother? "It's . . . uh, Ori. I'm going out for pizza with some girls from the volleyball team. Phil says Ms. W will give me a ride home. I . . . uh . . . just wanted you to know."

"Pizza?" Mom says like it's a foreign dish she's never heard of. "But I was planning to make dinner tonight. Claire gave me the evening off, and it's been a while since we've spent time together. I thought the two of us having dinner would be nice . . ."

Let's see. For about a hundred nights in a row, I've hung around the house alone with nothing to do. Now the one evening when I have plans, Mom decides we should bond over dinner. Not to mention that "nice" is not a word I'd use to describe the atmosphere when we're at home together.

"Sorry, Mom. I've already told the girls I'm going. This is only the second match we've won all season, and the first time I've gotten to play." I'm a little surprised at how proud I am of that. "Maybe some night next week?" But I can't imagine what we would talk about.

There's a long pause before she answers. "I'm sorry, too, but I want you to eat at home tonight. You'll have to go with the girls another time. Not for pizza, though. All that dough and cheese would wreak havoc with your complexion, not to mention your figure."

My complexion, my figure, my hair. Mom is still stuck on that same note. Has she ever seen me as a person? Or was I nothing more than a way for her to compete with her dead mother, glamorous Arianna?

"Did you hear what I said, Mom?" Anger is creeping into my voice. "I got to play in my first volleyball game ever and my team won. I want to celebrate with my friends." Okay, maybe they're not my friends yet, but—

"Fine," she snaps. "Go eat pizza. But don't come crying to me because your face is broken out and your jeans are too tight."

"Okay, Mom. And . . . I'll see you later." But I'm talking to a dial tone. "Oh, and don't worry, Mom," I

say to the dead line. "You're the last person I'd go crying to."

Half an hour later the five of us are tucked into a booth
at the Pizza Ranch. I'm sandwiched between Serena and
Mari who start chanting, "Prairie, prairie!" as soon as we
sit. Apparently, this is not something Phil and Shy want to
hear because they frown, shake their heads, and respond
with "Stampede!" Since I have no idea what's going on, I
keep my mouth shut and try to figure it out.

"Hold on, ladies!" Shy says, motioning for everyone to
be quiet. "None of us are going to change our minds. What
we need is a tiebreaker." She nods at me. "Looks like you're
it, Ori. What's it gonna be—stampede or prairie?"

My scalp tingles as all eyes turn to me. Serena and
Mari squeeze in closer and whisper "prairie" in my ears.
Phil and Shy reach across the table and try to push them
away from me. And, of course, they're saying the equally
meaningless word "stampede."

I squeeze my eyes shut and clap my hands over my
ears. "Stop it, everybody! I don't have a clue what you're
talking about!" When the noise and jostling stop, I lower
my hands and open my eyes. All four girls are staring at
me like I've sprouted an extra pair of ears.

Finally Phil says, "Ori's not a big pizza eater. I don't
think she's been here before. The 'prairie' is all veggies,
and the 'stampede' has four kinds of meat and veggies."

I've heard of sausage and pepperoni pizzas, but— "Four kinds of meat! Who eats four kinds of meat at the same time?"

Shy gives me an appraising look. "You have eaten pizza. Right?"

My face is getting hotter and hotter. "A few years ago my dance teacher took a group of us out for pizza after a dance rehearsal. But we all ordered plain cheese." I don't tell them how furious Mom was when she found out I'd eaten two slices.

Mari looks appalled. "So in your whole life you've only had pizza once?" Her long dark hair is damp, and the ends are frizzing.

"Ori, you are one pitiful creature," Shy says. She's wearing a bright yellow sweatshirt and gold hoop earrings that look wonderful with her dark skin. "Good thing we're here to teach you the ways of the world."

Serena turns in the seat so she's facing me. "We can definitely teach you the ways of pizza and ice cream and, well, pretty much any food that's fattening." Her lower lip is a little swollen from a collision with Phil's elbow when they were both going for the same shot. "Just don't expect us to help you hook up with guys."

"Speak for yourself, woman," Shy sniffs. "There's not a guy in the world who can stay away from all this."

Phil chuckles. "Really? Because based on what I've seen, the guys at Highland are using remarkable self-restraint."

"Watch your mouth!" Shy punches Phil in the arm. "I get more than my share of looks."

"Looks, maybe. Dates, no," Mari says. She plasters herself against the back of the booth out of Shy's reach.

Serena blows into her bangs. "Why are we wasting our time talking about guys when we could be eating pizza? Pizza is a delicious, cheesy treat. Guys are a pain in the rear end that I couldn't care less about."

"You said it, girl!" Mari reaches in front of me and slaps Serena's hand. Then they both reach across the table and slap Phil's. Thinking of my experience with Derrick, I hold my hands up to be slapped, too.

Shy puts her hands behind her back. "Nothing against you ladies, but I don't believe I'm ready to give up on the male gender."

"To each her own," Serena says with a grin. "But you don't know what you're missing." Before I realize what's happening, she plants a loud, wet kiss on my cheek. "Right, Ori?"

How much blood can rush into my head before it bursts like a blister?

"Uh, right," I manage to say. Because I'm *almost* completely sure she was just kidding.

38

Two days after my night out with the team I'm back in Phil's basement subjecting my muscles to more punishment. She starts us off with chin-ups, which I know are going to be a joke. Last week I could barely pull myself up one time, but Phil "helped" me do ten by holding my legs off the floor. When I was finished, my arms were so numb they felt like they were going to float away, and that was with Phil doing most of the work.

As usual, I stand watching in awe while Phil pulls herself up to the bar in the doorway of her workout room. Her stocky legs are bent, and she's stripped out of her sweatshirt to a threadbare Highland T-shirt. After twenty chin-ups, she drops lightly to the floor. "Okay, Ori. Show me what you've got."

I'm far from optimistic as I jump up and grab the bar. But I take a deep breath and let it out as I pull myself up.

"That's one!" Phil shouts as I touch the bar with my chin. I'm so excited that I almost lose my grip. "Come on, Ori!" I take another breath and pull again. "That's two!" My muscles are quivering, but I try again. On the third rep I'm short of the bar, and Phil helps me the rest of the way. And even though she gives me a lot of assistance on the last seven chin-ups, I'm feeling great when my feet hit the floor after number ten.

"Good job, Ori!" Phil is smiling when she pats my shoulder. "You're making excellent progress! Keep it up, and someday I might have to stop calling you a wuss."

"Thanks, but 'wuss' is still going to fit for a long time." I try not to flinch as I rub out the cramp in my left bicep. Phil does another set of fifteen chin-ups, but my arms have had it.

We switch to bent-over dumbbell rows, which are much easier because I'm lifting twelve-pound dumbbells instead of my body weight. Phil is using thirties, but I'll never be as strong as she is, so there's no use comparing myself to her.

"Do any of the other volleyball girls ever work out here with you?" I ask while we take a stretch break between sets, which we do by hanging from the chin bar. I've done my thirty seconds, and now Phil is swaying back and forth as if she'd be comfortable hanging there all day.

"Shy and Mari ride their bikes over when the weather's

decent, but Serena lives too far," Phil says. She lets go of the bar and walks over to take a drink from her water bottle. "When Shy gets her license next month, all of them will probably be here every day."

"I like your friends. And you all get along so well." I've had two days to think about the kiss thing, and I've concluded that it was almost definitely a joke.

Phil wipes her mouth with the hem of her T-shirt. "Mari and Serena have been tight since elementary school. And Shy is in so many activities that she's going a dozen directions at once. But, yeah, we're all good friends."

"I'm surprised Ms. W hasn't snapped Shy up as a client. With her height and bone structure, she has modeling potential. Of course, she'd need to lose at least twenty pounds."

Phil doesn't answer. Instead she picks up the thirty-pound dumbbells and begins another set of bent-over rows. I sigh and pick my weights up, too. When Phil's working out, it's hard to distract her, although that doesn't stop me from trying.

But when we finish our sets, Phil sits on a workout bench instead of stretching. She looks at me, shaking her head like a photographer who can't get a little kid to pose the way he wants. "Do you remember what you just said?"

I collapse onto the other bench and search my brain, but I draw a blank. "Just now?"

"Yeah, just now." There's more than a hint of sarcasm in her voice. "The comment you made about Shy."

"I said she has potential as a model, didn't I?" Which doesn't seem like a reason for Phil to be getting bitchy with me.

"You also said she needs to lose twenty pounds," Phil pounces as if she's caught me in a major lie.

"So? If she's interested in modeling, she'll need to lose at least that much." Now I'm getting irritated. "I was just making an observation."

"See, Ori, that's the problem." Phil scratches a dry patch on her elbow. She should start using a skin cream with richer emollients.

"Yesterday morning you 'made an observation' to me that Serena's roots were showing. A few minutes later you 'observed' that Mari should get braces on her lower teeth—and have her eyebrows waxed, too. And after school today you pointed out that Ceci's skirt was too tight across her butt."

My stomach drops. "Oh, no! Did one of them hear me?"

"Not this time." Phil shakes her head. "But that's not my point." She takes a deep breath, and I realize she's uncomfortable about saying whatever she's going to say. Which causes an uneasy flutter in my stomach. "Ori, you spend way too much time focusing on other people's flaws."

"What do you mean?" I reach for a strand of hair to twist before I remember and let my hand drop into my lap. "Everyone focuses on the way people look. Even you."

Phil gulps some more water. "Sure, I notice how people look. It's pretty hard not to. But you . . . well . . . you pass judgment."

"No, I don't." My defenses are coming up. "I just think of ways people could make themselves look better."

Phil leans forward with her elbows on her knees. "Look, Ori. I'm not saying you're a bad person. In the modeling world, picking other girls apart is natural. But it's holding you back from really making friends."

"How?" Just when I thought I was starting to fit in, Phil tells me I'm still doing it all wrong.

"Because when you're assessing people's looks, you can't appreciate them for themselves," Phil says. "When you get a birthday present, what's more important—the shiny wrapping paper or what's inside?"

"I know, 'Looks don't matter. It's what's inside that counts.' Try telling that to a modeling scout." Before Phil jumps up and strangles me, I add, "I probably do pay more attention to appearance than some—maybe most— people. But I'm aware of their personalities."

Phil gives me an *I've gotcha now* grin. "Okay, let's see you prove it. You've spent some time around Shy. Describe her without saying a word about her appearance."

How hard can that be? I close my eyes to bring Shy into focus. First, there's her regal posture, especially the way she holds her chin up. Wait. Posture is part of appearance. Eyes, nose, hair, and figure are all off limits. "How about this? Shy has a deep voice, and—"

"Appearance," Phil cuts me off.

I could argue the point, but Phil would get the last word like she always does. "Shy is popular"—Phil's forehead creases, and I know she's ready to stop me again—"because she has lots of self-confidence. She says what's on her mind and doesn't worry about whether somebody gets offended. But she lets other people say what's on their minds, too."

I'm out of breath, like I just did ten chin-ups. It was harder to find my way to Shy's personality than I thought it would be.

"Not that easy, is it?" Phil says. "But, just like exercise, the more you look beyond the wrapping paper to the person inside, the easier it gets."

Phil may be right. But for someone like me who's spent her whole life designing wrapping paper, it's not going to be easy.

At our next volleyball match, Coach Boston puts the original starters back in. But she gives me three minutes of playing time in both the second and third games even though we're not that far ahead. I don't commit any fouls, make a few assists, and even bump a shot over the net. Still, it's going to be a long time before the starters have anything to worry about from me.

After the match—which we barely pull out in the last game—we hold the usual mass celebration. Although I still haven't gotten used to being hugged and smacked by sweaty, stinky girls, I don't mind it as much as I did at first.

A few weeks ago you couldn't have dragged me into the school showers. But everyone on the team showers in the locker room, so I overlook the mold, scum, and yuckiness for the thirty seconds it takes to jump in and get wet. The shower I take when I get home is my secret. And, while the other girls have to cope with wet, frizzy hair, my head comes out nice and shiny.

Which is why I'm out of the locker room and on my way home before everyone else. Phil invited me to go to a movie with her and Ms. W, but I declined. I'm not ready to see them being all mother/daughter. Not when Mom hasn't spoken my name in days.

"Look, Gypsy, it's a guy from the swim team. Aren't his broad shoulders and manly muscles awesome?" Morgan appears from behind the open gym door like a gorilla from the mist. Two humps of zit-dotted cleavage pop out of a bright blue V-neck sweater that's stretched like Saran Wrap over her muffin-top stomach roll.

"That's crude, Morgan. Just leave her alone." Gypsy's eyes skip over me, and she starts down the hall toward the exit. "Derrick and the guys are waiting out front."

"Ohmygod!" Morgan makes big, surprised eyes. "I was *so sure* it was a guy, but it's Oribaldie. She's turned into a volleyball jock like her new *superclose* friend, Phil."

"What's that supposed to mean?" The words grind out

between my teeth. I usually give Morgan's insults the attention I do to buzzing gnats, but Phil is off limits.

"Let's see. You shaved your head—*like a guy*—joined the volleyball team, and you've got muscles popping out all over." Morgan tugs her sweater down, which is like trying to cover a school bus with a napkin. "You hang out twenty-four/seven with Phil, the megajock team captain. It's simple math—even for you."

The exit doors open, and an icy blast of wind chills the damp skin on the back of my head. I shiver.

"Get it in gear, Morgue, or we're leaving without you!" Derrick bellows from the end of the hall.

"On my way!" Morgan lifts her arm and waves, giving me a view of the doughy flesh around her waist. "Figure it out, Oribaldie. For someone who looks like Phil, an ex-beauty queen, even a bald one, is quite a prize."

She jiggles away, leaving me standing in the hall with my mouth open and my thoughts scrambled.

At home I try to read *Pride and Prejudice* for English Lit, but all I think about is Phil. I've never totally let go of the idea that some of the volleyball girls might be gay, but it never crossed my mind that Phil might be attracted to me. She doesn't seem to like me that way, but how would I know? She's the first friend I've had. What if she has a crush on me? How can I tell her I'm not interested without hurting her feelings—and losing her friendship?

I am so out of my depth. Sit five pageant judges in front of me, and I'll feed them the answers they want to hear. Hand me a script, and I'll slip into the character's skin like it's a comfortable pair of jeans. But ask me to do a simple thing, like being a friend, and I'm lost.

I wonder if other girls discuss dilemmas like this with their mothers. Mom and I used to talk constantly, but our conversations were always about my career. Not having a social life, I didn't have any personal problems to discuss. And if Mom had issues, I never heard about them. How could we spend all that time together and be strangers?

Just as I'm thinking about Mom, she knocks on my bedroom door.

"It's unlocked." Until my life caved into a sinkhole, I didn't spend much time in my room. And almost never with the door closed.

"Oh, you're doing homework." Mom's wearing her favorite dark blue suit—the one that brings out her eyes. Her face sags with that weary, hopeless look I'm sick of seeing. *I'm hairless, Mother, not deceased.* "This will only take a minute."

I set the book on my desk without bothering to mark the place. I'll have to reread the chapter anyway.

"I don't know if you remember, but you have a recheck with Dr. Fazio in two weeks." She's standing just outside the doorway like a vampire who can't come in without being invited.

The volleyball schedule is thumbtacked on the corkboard above my desk. "On a Friday afternoon?"

Mom rushes ahead like she's practiced this speech and

228 @ JAN BLAZANIN

doesn't want to forget it. "Yes, and I was thinking if you stop shaving your head, he'll be able to tell how much new growth there is—"

I'm shaking my head, but she doesn't notice. "I have a volleyball game that day."

"I'm sure somebody can take your place."

I knew that's what she'd say. "That's not the point. My team is playing, and I need to be there." She tries to interrupt, but I keep talking. "If you want to reschedule my appointment for a day when I don't have a game—or practice—I'll go. But the treatments are worthless."

"How can you tell anything with your head shaved?" She's twisting her wedding ring around her finger like she does when she's upset.

"I only shave my head three times a week." *You might notice if you ever looked at me.* "Every morning when I get up and every night before I go to bed I study myself in my magnifying mirror. And every morning and every night I feel all over my scalp, especially around the little dents where I had the shots." *And every morning and every night hope drains from my heart.* "I am not growing any hair."

"Then we'll ask Dr. Fazio to try a different treatment. I've read some promising things about photochemotherapy. Doctors are also using squaric acid and—"

Acid? Chemotherapy?

"Treatments, treatments, treatments! That's all you ever talk about!" As I jump up, my desk chair tips over backward. I kick it out of the way. "Do you even care how awful this has been for me?"

"Of course I care. You're my daughter. But—"

"Then, why haven't you asked how I'm feeling? How I'm doing in school? If I've made any friends?"

"You're having side effects again?" Mom frowns. "You haven't said anything."

I have better communication with my toothbrush. "Except for the obvious, I'm fine physically."

"Then what?" Mom looks baffled. "I've never known you to care about your grades, or having friends."

"That was before. In case you haven't noticed, things have changed." I'd like to smash something, but instead I set my chair back on its legs.

"We're both upset about this . . . setback in your career." Her voice is sweet enough to rot my teeth. "But I know we'll find the right treatment, and once we're on track again—"

"Stop it!" I'm so frustrated I could shake her. "I don't need more treatments. I need you to listen to me. And look at me—bald head and all. I need you to be my mother."

"Oribella, stop being so dramatic." Mom puts her hands on her hips. "I look at you every day, and it pains me to see you throw away your life's work when we haven't begun to explore all the options."

"I'm talking about exploring my options. Maybe I want to do other things besides—"

"Such as?" she snaps. The edges of her lips are white.

"Such as playing volleyball and having friends and getting good grades." I lower myself into my desk chair because my legs are trembling. "Dad graduated from Iowa State with honors. Don't you think he'd want me to do well in school?"

Mom's expression is somewhere between pain and anger. "What your father would or wouldn't want is immaterial. I'm the one who raised you." She clasps her hands as if she's trying to calm herself. "You and I have always been partners with one goal—one dream. It makes me sick that you're letting it die."

I rub my temples in frustration. "That's what I'm trying to say, Mom. I don't need a partner anymore. I need you to support my dreams no matter what they are."

For a moment Mom lowers her face into her hands. When she raises her head, she looks as tired as death. "Those aren't dreams. All you're doing is settling for the ordinary."

With a sad shake of her head, Mom walks out of my room and closes the door behind her.

39

"*Y*ou've *never* been to a sleepover?" Phil's eyebrows disappear under the hem of her ugly pink and green hat. The frayed yarn is end-of-the-winter grungy.

Ms. W glances at us in the rearview mirror, and I'm reminded of riding with Mom in the backseat of Miles Crawford's limousine. I lost my movie contract months and months ago, but the memories still cut to the bone.

"And that surprises you why?" My hands are folded in my lap so Phil can't see them shaking. Now, if my sweaty palms don't leave a wet mark on my coat . . .

It's a sleepover at Phil's, not Death Row. So what if she's gay? So what if they're all gay? They're the same people you liked before Morgan shot off her canyon-size mouth.

"Okay, I'm not surprised. Just go with the flow, and you'll be fine."

"Oribella," Ms. W says, "I received the molding kit from Locks of Love. We can make a plaster cast of your head tomorrow morning and order your fit cap right away. The sooner you're fitted, the sooner your wig will arrive."

My brain is buzzing. It's been weeks since Ms. W mentioned the wig, and—figuring it would never happen—I put it out of my mind. People have gotten used to seeing me bald. Will wearing a wig make me look like a phony?

"Wig!" Phil bounces off the seat. "You're going to cover my handiwork?"

"We're going to allow Oribella to explore all her options." Ms. W turns the car into her driveway. "Right, dear?"

I manage to nod and smile, but I'm thinking of the rumors about the volleyball team. I'd rather leave some options unexplored.

"Don't run into the woods, you moron!" Mari's knees are drawn up to her chin, and she's peeking through her fingers at the screen. Her long hair, caught in a scrunchie on top of her head, spills around her face like a dark fountain.

The team lets out a collective groan as the blond cheerleader, barefoot in a lacy white teddy, runs screaming into the forest.

"Now she'll trip. Wait for it. Wait for it." Destiny's

glasses are barely caught on the tip of her nose, and she's waving a half-eaten slice of cheese pizza like a baton. "And she's down!"

Black slime oozes over the cheerleader, sucking away her skin and bones, reducing the once-beautiful girl to a mushy red puddle.

"Now that is just nasty!" Shy shakes her head.

Phil holds up a bag of tortilla chips. "Hey, Ori, pass the salsa over here. This is making me hungry."

"You're disgusting!" Mari covers her face with a throw pillow.

I lift the bowl of salsa over Mari's head and hand it to Phil. The girls are so easy with each other. I wish I could quit worrying and just relax.

Phil scoops a glob of salsa onto a tortilla chip and shoves it into her mouth. "Umm! Blood and entrails. Delicious!"

"Movie time is over!" Mari grabs the remote off the sofa and hits the stop button. "Let's do something else."

"Oh, come on. It was just getting to the good part." Phil lunges for the remote, but Mari tosses it to Shy.

"That movie has no good part." Serena yawns, showing her crooked bottom teeth.

When I decided to take Phil's advice and stop focusing on other people's flaws, I didn't know it would be such a tough habit to break.

Serena sits cross-legged on the sofa. "Let's gossip instead."

Destiny slides another piece of pizza out of the box. "Now that's entertainment! You first."

"No. Ori goes first." Shy turns on me with a stare that makes my mouth go dry. "You haven't said boo all night, and you've been eyeing us like a guppy in a tank of sharks. You got something on your mind, say it."

My breath stops. My heart stops.

Serena, Destiny, and Mari squint at me like I'm a suspect in a police lineup. It's so quiet I can hear branches scraping against the brick siding.

"Go on, Ori, confess." Phil's smile takes in all of us. "It's her first sleepover. Ever."

"That's it? You're scared of spending the night away from Momma?" Shy's tone is somewhere between suspicious and teasing.

I feel like she just poked an old bruise. "Momma" and I couldn't be more apart if I lived on the moon.

Everyone waits while I study the floor. I could agree with Phil, but my uneasiness would always separate me from the rest of the team. I've had a lifetime of that.

"Not exactly. No. Not really. I mean, yes, it's my first sleepover." I'm stumbling like a three-year-old in her mom's high heels. "But, it's . . . I like you girls and all, but . . . I'm not gay."

Mari rotates her head in an exaggerated swoop. "Is it just me, or did that come out of nowhere?"

"About a hundred miles beyond nowhere." Serena steeples her fingers under her chin and looks at me through her blond bangs. "But thanks for sharing, Ori."

"Yeah. Good to know . . . I guess." Mari twirls her geyser ponytail into a braid. "But, why did you feel the need to share that little tidbit with us?"

"Because we're jocks, and all jocks are lesbians. Right, Oribella?" Phil's voice is flat, and her face has turned a dull red.

"You think we're gay? Oh, this is too funny!" Shy bursts out laughing. "Where did you get that news bite?"

Phil's pained expression makes my stomach ache.

"See, when we were at the Pizza Ranch, Mari said you weren't interested in guys. And then Serena kissed me on the cheek. But I still thought you were kidding until Morgan said . . ." The sentence dies. Because listening to Morgan was beyond stupid.

"Morgan?" Shy rolls onto her back laughing and kicks her long legs in the air. "Now there's a reliable source!"

Serena slides her arm around Mari's shoulders. "Kiss me, you red-hot thing!" She puckers her lips like a fish.

"Stop! It's not funny!" Phil yells. Her face is purple with anger.

Serena pulls her arm away. "Oh, Phil, I think—"

But Phil pounds up the stairs before Serena can finish her thought.

My mouth should be surgically sealed.

I'm on my feet and after Phil while the stairs are still vibrating.

"Ori, wait!" Serena calls after me. "Phil's temper is—"

Phil's temper is not my worry right now. If she punches me in the nose, I deserve it. Well, maybe not the nose. . . .

Phil runs into Ms. W's reception room and flops face-down on the black leather sofa. Her jeans' pockets are worn through, and her sweatshirt was burgundy a few centuries ago. She looks like a little boy with a Buster Brown haircut.

I just did it again.

"Phil, I'm sorry. That was a stupid, stupid thing for me to say." Her shoulders are shaking, but I can't tell if she's crying. "It doesn't matter, and it's none of my business and . . . I wish I'd kept my mouth shut."

"Why? You'd still be thinking it." The sofa muffles Phil's voice. "Phil's a jock; she looks like a guy. Of course she's a lesbian."

"You don't look like a guy. You're just not into . . ." I don't know how to finish the sentence without hurting her feelings even more.

"I'm just not into looking attractive. Isn't that what you're trying to say?" Phil finishes for me. "You should know, since you're the expert on how people should look."

I wince, but I can't blame her for being pissed at me. I have to find the words to make it right. "Phil, you're the most beautiful person I know. You helped me through . . . things I couldn't have survived without you. And you're a better friend to me than I thought anyone could be. None of the rest of it matters."

"It matters to me!" Phil rolls over and sits up. Her cheeks flame where they were stuck to the sofa, but her eyes are dry. "Just because I look—like I do—everybody thinks I'm not interested in guys." Looking miserable, she drags her fingers through her hair. "But I am interested. Oh, what's the point?"

The truth dawns on me. "It's not *guys*. It's *a guy*! Who is he?"

Phil jumps up and stalks to the end of the waiting room. She stops, turns, and stalks back. "Like I said, what's the point? My hair is boring, my face is a zero, and I'm shaped like a trash can."

"That is not true. Okay, your hair could use an update," I concede, "but you have great eyes, a knockout smile, and cute dimples."

Phil sinks back onto the sofa. "You've just described my five-year-old cousin Sean. Except he has more curves."

"There's nothing wrong with your body, Phil." I sit on the other end of the sofa, in case she decides to punch me after all. "But your clothes are . . . awful. *They* make your shape look like a trash can."

She doesn't hit me, so I plunge ahead. "I don't know much about sleepovers—"

"That came out loud and clear." The corner of Phil's mouth slants up. "Here's Rule Number One: Don't announce that you're not gay. It gives the impression you think we're sexual predators."

"No chance of me forgetting." I'm weak with relief

that Phil is actually smiling. "There are a lot of things I'm not good at—social functions being primary—but I have some skills. If you'd let me—"

"No, you don't!" Phil holds up her hands and backs into the corner of the sofa. "Mom tried it; it doesn't work. I cannot be made over."

"And when was that? Two years ago? Three?" I play my ace card. "I let you shave my head. The least you can do is let me give you a makeover."

"Makeover! Makeover!" Serena stands in the doorway hopping up and down like a little kid. "Me, too!" The other girls, who are clustered behind her, all nod.

"Yah, we want to look good for the ladies," Shy says with a wink.

Phil sighs. "I'll go ask Mom if we can use her studio."

Ms. W's studio is a makeup artist's dream. Along two walls are mirrored makeup stations, each equipped with samples of blush, foundation, eyeliner, shadow, hair products, twist curlers, and pretty much anything else you could want. Ms. W has connections in the cosmetics industry that supply her with all the trendiest products. The suppliers figure if Ms. W's clients like the samples, they're going to buy more and tell their friends, too. And, speaking from personal experience, they're right.

I've been in here a thousand times but never with anyone as excited as Mari, Serena, and Destiny. They practically knocked Phil down rushing through the door. For the past few minutes, they've been dashing from station to station, exclaiming over the samples as if they've discovered a diamond mine.

Shy is standing just inside the door where she's out of danger from their flying arms and legs. We look at each other and smile like indulgent parents. Phil, who's leaning against the wall, clearly would rather be on the volleyball court, in the weight room, or anywhere but here.

"Okay, Ori. You started this," she says. "It's your job to get these maniacs under control before they break something."

Using Ms. Summers' technique, I clap my hands. "Mari! Serena! Destiny! Time to get glamorous!"

They turn in midstride, sprint over, and skid to a stop in front of me. "Here we are," Destiny pants. Her wavy black hair swirls around her face and her dark, freckled cheeks are flushed. "Make us beautiful."

As I look at their expectant faces, my mouth goes dry. They're waiting for me to tell them what to do, which is completely out of my realm. I'm used to following directions. Giving directions to other people is uncharted territory.

But so is the rest of my life.

"All right, ladies, a makeover begins with hair. The best way to go is with partners who will each shampoo and style the other one's hair. Since my hair is already perfect"—I rub my smooth scalp—"my partner will have it easy."

"Then I call Ori!" Phil launches herself away from the wall and grabs my arm.

Destiny rolls her eyes. "What a slacker!" But she's already carrying an extra makeup stool to the station where Shy is standing. Mari and Serena choose the station to Shy's left. When Shy turns to talk to Destiny, Mari tries to snatch a pot of their lip gloss.

"Keep your itchy fingers off our products," Shy says, blocking Mari with her body. "Or you'll be sporting an Oribella haircut at school on Monday."

Mari sticks out her tongue. "Ooh! I'm so scared!" But she slides behind Serena.

I do the hand-clap thing again. "Okay, everybody. First we shampoo and condition."

The six of us troop over to the three beauty salon sinks on the far wall. As the air fills with steam and the flowery fragrance of shampoo, an ache builds in my chest. Some of the models I used to work with complained about the time they spent taking care of their hair, but I loved washing and conditioning mine, brushing it, trying out new styles. I miss the weight of it hanging down my back.

"Hey!" Mari shouts. I look up from washing Phil's hair to see Mari wiping shampoo suds from her face. Shy is standing at the next sink with a handful of lather and an innocent look on her face.

"It is so on!" Mari flings a handful of foam at Shy, who bobs out of the way.

Destiny, leaning back in the sink, gets a mouthful of froth. Spitting soap, she jumps up and sloshes water on the floor. "What the hell?"

Shy points her finger at Mari. "Mari did it!" she shouts and scoops up more bubbles to toss.

"But Shy started it!" Mari protests.

"And I'm stopping it!" Phil bellows. "If Mom's cleaning lady quits because you guys made a mess in here, guess who'll be doing our cleaning?" As she sits up, I wrap a towel around her head to keep her hair from dripping. "Here's a hint—it won't be me."

"Oops! Sorry." Mari swipes at the wet floor with a towel. "But Shy—" She sees Phil's frown and gulps back the rest. "Never mind. The shampoo war is officially over."

When I finish shampooing Phil's hair, we go back to the makeup station. "I don't have much experience at haircutting," I tell her, "but I could probably even up your ends a little."

Phil shrugs. "Go for it. I doubt you can make it look worse."

"If you don't like your cut, why don't you change stylists?" I ask as I snip tentatively at her ragged ends. Then I see her sheepish expression. "Please tell me you did not cut your own hair!"

Another shrug. "I was too busy to fit a hair appointment around the volleyball schedule. And it didn't seem like trimming my hair would be that hard."

I resist the urge to smack Phil on the head. "It's a shame you don't have, say, a mother in the beauty business who could help you out."

"Okay, fine," she grumbles. "Next time I'll have one of those walk-in places cut it."

"No, Philomena. Next time I'll get you an appointment with my stylist. I'm positive she has at least one opening in her schedule."

By the time I finish trimming Phil's hair, the second girl of each team is busily braiding, spritzing, or curling her partner's hair. Since Phil's hair is short and layered— thanks to her jagged cutting—I set it on sponge rollers.

When I've finished setting Phil's hair, she stands up and motions for me to sit on the makeup stool. "In case you haven't noticed, Phil, I don't have anything to style."

With a grin I can only describe as devilish, Phil picks up an eyeliner pencil. Holding it in the air, she looks at the other girls. "Don't worry, Ori. I'm sure your girl-loving teammates can come up with something."

"Quit wriggling around, or I'm going to poke eyeliner in your eye." I'm holding Phil's face with my left hand, but she's tossing her head like a wild horse.

"I told you not to put it on me. I'll never wear it." With

her hair wound up in pink and blue rollers, Phil already looks sexier. "Mascara is my limit."

I'm not giving up that easily. "Mascara *and* eye shadow. That's my best offer."

"Hey, Ori! Am I doing this right?" Mari is steadying Destiny's head and filling in her eyebrows with pencil.

Destiny looks over at me. "After the practice we had on Ori's head, we're pros."

I stop making up Phil's eyes to check myself in the mirror. Thanks to my teammates, my head is covered with graffiti. Along the arch where my hairline used to be, it says, "Volleyball girls are guy magnets!" in turquoise and rose eyeliner. The sides and back of my head are covered with a rainbow of similar slogans.

I throw my head back and strike a pose. "I look gorgeous."

Shy wags a tube of lip liner at me. "And . . . what did you learn from this experience?"

I rest my left hand on the rollers in Phil's hair and raise my right hand. "I swear on Phil's head—and this Dazzling Amber mascara wand—that I will never believe *any* gossip about my volleyball teammates. *And* I will never, ever, ever listen to Morgan."

"Because if you do," Phil says, "we break out the Sharpies."

40

By the time Ms. W drops me off at home, it's Saturday noon. We waited for everybody to leave before Ms. W made the mold of my head. When she took it off, we laughed ourselves silly at what the Locks of Love people would think when they saw my head graffiti inside it.

It's one of those beautiful end-of-March days that makes living in Iowa seem like a decent idea. The sky—a deep, new-spring blue—sets off the cotton-ball clouds and tiny, almost-open leaves. The sun warms my head, reminding me of all I've lost. But what I've found lightens my steps.

Mom works on Saturdays, so I'm surprised her car is in the driveway. I hate how my stomach lurches at the thought of being home with her all afternoon. When was the last time I looked forward to spending time with her?

Music is coming from the living room—a lame tune from Mom's high school days. I used to tease her about her CDs all the time, but it's been months since she's played her music. And teasing . . . I can't remember when.

I hold the door so it doesn't slam and give me away. But Mom's dusting the small table just around the corner where she leaves her keys and purse. I'd have to be invisible to sneak past her.

"Hello, prin—" When she catches herself, pain twists a knot in my stomach. Why doesn't she just hold up a sign that reads, Guess What? I Don't Love You? Her mouth pulls into an unconvincing smile. "Did you have a nice time at Philomena's?"

"She goes by Phil." I switch my overnight bag to my left shoulder and maneuver through the hall. Mom and her dustcloth are taking up half the entryway, so I can't get past without brushing against her.

"What are those marks on your head?"

"Don't worry, Mother, it's not a new deformity." Mom's mouth tightens. My nasty remark hit its target. "The volleyball girls were messing around."

"This volleyball . . . do you like it?" If the dustcloth were a person, she'd be strangling it to death. She's avoided me ever since I stopped the treatments. Why pretend she cares now?

"It's exercise. I've made friends. Yeah, I like it. But the

season ends in two weeks, so . . ." I try not to think about that.

"It suits you, I think. You look . . . robust."

"Robust?" A laugh escapes me. "Aren't you confusing me with coffee?"

Mom's eyes light up. "Okay, not quite the right word. You look healthy, even blooming."

Blooming. Maybe I am—a little. Like a flower after a long, bleak winter.

"When the season is over . . ." Mom bites her lower lip. "Have you thought about going to back to dance class?"

Every day.

"I've missed too many lessons now. . . ." And I can't face Ms. Summers' pity and Gypsy's satisfied smirk.

"I thought maybe . . . you seemed to love it so much." The light goes out of Mom's eyes, and her cheeks hang in tired folds. I won't feel sorry for her.

I've learned to live without a lot of things I loved.

"The school e-mailed your midterm grades to me. Apparently, it's something new they're doing this semester." She wipes her hands on her housework sweatshirt as if her palms are sweating.

Does talking to me make her that uncomfortable?

"You scored eighty-seven percent in algebra." Her eyes get a faraway look. "Lee would be so proud of you. He found math endlessly fascinating. She chuckles a little. "In that respect we were exact opposites."

How does she dare to talk about Dad? "Not that long

ago you told me that what Dad would have wanted is immaterial."

Mom's smile dissolves. "At the time I was angry and disappointed, but I should never have said that. Your dad adored you. And in my heart I believe he's watching over both of us every day."

I step around her to keep her from seeing the wetness in my eyes. "I didn't get any sleep last night. I'm going to bed."

"Oh. I thought maybe . . ." The dustcloth dangles from Mom's hand.

In spite of myself, I wait.

"I'm starting a new job Monday—office manager in an insurance company in West Des Moines. They're paying me five dollars an hour more than I was getting at Bonds and Butterfly Boutique combined plus vacation, sick leave, insurance. And no weekends." Her eyes ask me for something. Approval?

I won't give it to her. "I thought you liked working weekends. You know, less time to spend with the freak."

Mom winces. "I know I've handled this—your situation—all wrong. I haven't supported you the way I should have. I hoped—"

My situation? "You dumped me like a sack of garbage." The strap of my overnight bag bites into my shoulder, but that pain is minor. "You're my mother. You're supposed to love *me*—not the way I look. But you can't stand the sight of me."

"That's not the way I—" She looks away. "I-I've been seeing someone, Oribella."

My spine goes rigid, and I feel the blood drain from my face. I guess that explains why she's gone all the time.

"No, I said that wrong," Mom hurries to explain. "I'm not dating. For the past several weeks I've been talking to a counselor."

I swallow my surprise. That's the last thing I expected her to say.

"She's helping me face some things about myself that aren't terribly pleasant."

I could list some things about Mom that aren't terribly pleasant, too, but I keep my mouth closed.

"Actually, she's a family counselor." Mom is choking the dustcloth again. "And she'd like to meet with both of us, together as well as separately. She thinks that talking everything out will help us . . . well, get past what's happened."

"I don't get it." I'm fighting to keep my voice from breaking. "For months and months I've tried to talk to you, and all you've done is shut me out. Now you and this counselor decide we should share our feelings, and I'm supposed to be grateful that you finally have time for me.

"You blew all your chances, Mother. So don't wait for me to show at your next session."

"I'm so sorry. The way I treated you was horribly, horribly wrong." Mom's eyes fill with tears. "Can't we—"

"I'm going to bed," I cut her off.

I sprint upstairs, my overnight bag banging against my back. As I close my bedroom door, I hear, "Sleep tight."

But I don't sleep. So what if Mom said she was sorry? She couldn't say she loves me. Maybe that was too much of a lie, even for her.

I lie awake—dry-eyed—listening to Mom's music all afternoon and into the evening.

41

*P*hil wears her new look to school Monday morning. With her brown hair in a curly bob, her eyes highlighted with a touch of makeup, and a tucked-in V-neck sweater and belted jeans showing off her toned body, she's a poster girl for glowing good health.

I'm walking over to congratulate Phil for her bravery when SUV Guy—Dwayne Overstreet, who is her secret crush—cuts me off. He's replaced the peace sign in his hair with a lightning bolt. And from the look on Phil's face when he smiles at her, I'd say the lightning bolt has struck both of them.

Phil sees me and smiles, but I just wave. She doesn't need me tagging along.

When I turn my head, Gypsy is standing beside me. She's had her hair cut. It falls in waves to just above her shoulders, accenting her deep brown eyes and slanting cheekbones. And she's wearing a boxy red plaid jacket that's perfect for her coloring.

I jump like a cat and check the hallway, but Gypsy seems to be without her roving swarm of skanks. "Phil looks great, doesn't she?" I have no good reason for saying it, except Phil does, and I'm proud of her.

Gypsy tucks a lock of hair behind her ear, revealing tiny pearl earrings. "Several of the volleyball girls look sharp today. You always did have a sense of style."

"Thanks." Gypsy usually puts as much distance between us as possible. The oddness of standing here talking to her makes me feel like a deer in the headlights; I know the car is going to hit me, but I can't move. People stare as they walk around us, expecting a catfight. They won't get one from me.

Gypsy holds her notebook against her chest like a shield and shifts from one foot to the other. "We're never going to be friends."

You stopped to tell me that?

"But I've said things . . . about, you know . . . that weren't right, and I'm sorry." She levels her eyes at me. "You've handled . . . your hair loss . . . a lot better than I ever could. I respect that."

I let out the breath I've been holding. "Thanks."

"Well . . . that's all I had to say." Gypsy touches her hair. "Except . . . when I got my hair cut, I donated it to Locks of Love. I hope it helps."

As she walks down the hall, I whisper, "Thanks," my word for the day.

My horoscope must say I'm going to renew old acquaintances today, because I'm sitting at the bus stop after volleyball practice when Ms. Summers cruises past in a blue convertible. I wouldn't notice her except she has the top down even though it's only about fifty degrees, and she's waving a scarf and calling, "Yoo-hoo! Oribella!"

I've never heard anyone say "Yoo-hoo" except in the movies, but it's so Ms. Summers. I laugh and wave back. She does a U-turn in the middle of traffic, screeches to a stop at the curb, and jumps out of her car.

"Oribella! It's wonderful to see you!" Ms. Summers hugs me against her bony chest, and her tweed jacket scratches my cheek. She smells like talcum powder and muscle rub and sweat. My legs nearly buckle from homesickness.

Ms. Summers holds me at arm's length. "You look incredible! And what muscle tone!" Her fingers are digging into my shoulders, but I don't mind at all. "Confess! You've been lifting weights."

"And playing volleyball."

"Yes, I heard!" She's so close I can see the dark pores in her nose and the little lines—

Forget what she looks like and listen.

"It's wonderful exercise, and it obviously suits you. But

a little bird told me the season is nearly over." She gives me a sly smile. "It's time to return to your dancing."

A little bird? "I've missed too many classes. I don't know the routines—" My need to dance is a constant ache.

Ms. Summers brushes aside my protests. "That's why you and I will start with private lessons. You'll be in top form in a matter of a few weeks."

Private lessons. Nobody staring. But . . . "The money—"

"Not to worry. You're paid up for months in advance."

"I am?" My excuses are flying out the window.

"Rhonda has been on the automatic payment plan for years," Ms. Summers says. "When you weren't coming to class, I contacted her about stopping the payments, but she wanted to continue." She takes my hands. "She was sure you'd come back."

Mom could have saved six hundred dollars a month by stopping those payments. Instead she worked extra hours, weekends, to pay the bills.

"And you will, won't you?" Ms. Summers squeezes my fingers. "I have Wednesdays at five o'clock."

A warm feeling, sweet as melted chocolate, pours through me. "Yes, I will."

42

*P*hil bumps the ball to me, and I punch it over the net. The Hoover team sends it sailing back. Serena attacks, and the ball lands untouched in the middle of the opposite court. Point for our team.

Hoover calls a time-out. Coach Boston waves us to the sidelines, pulls me out, and puts Jessica back in. Being benched for the last five minutes is a letdown, but I'm glad Coach gave me court time in our last game. I'm still not starter material, but that won't stop me from trying out next year.

While Coach discusses strategy, I gulp a bottle of water, and my eyes wander to the bleachers. Sophomore girls' volleyball doesn't have much of a following, so the stands are almost empty. The tall blond in the red coat picking her way down the steps is impossible to miss.

Water catches halfway down my throat, sending me into a coughing fit. By the time I look up, the blond is walking out the exit. I didn't see her up close, but I could never mistake her hair, her walk, or her favorite spring coat.

We win the last game and match, and I bounce and shriek with the rest of the Highland team. But our victory is not on my mind. Because, after all these months, the hard knot of anger in my chest is unraveling. Mom took time off from her new job to watch me play volleyball. She's been paying for my dance lessons.

Mom is trying to reach out to me. Maybe it's time to reach back.

If only I knew how.

When Ms. W calls Tuesday evening to tell me my "fit cap" has arrived from Locks of Love, I'm ridiculously happy to hear her voice. Although it's been less than a week since the season ended, I feel lost without volleyball, and my dance lessons with Ms. Summers don't start until tomorrow. Phil assures me we'll still spend time together, but between her track practice and Dwayne, I'm not sure where I'll fit in.

"This is the exciting part: selecting the color and length of your wig," Ms. W says. She's as giggly as a little girl.

"What about black hair?" I tease. "With silver streaks."

Ms. W chuckles. "I'm sure that would be charming. But perhaps you'd prefer something closer to your natural color."

I pretend to pout. "I suppose I can live with light green. But I still want silver streaks."

"Of course you do, dear. I'll pick you up in fifteen minutes."

I look down at the ratty sweats I'm wearing and dash upstairs to change. Ms. W is still Ms. W, and old habits are hard to break.

On the way to my room I remember my bag of hair and detour into my bathroom. I can use it to find a perfect match for my color. I kneel and rummage under the sink.

My poor, poor hair. What I'd give to have it back. I open the bag and press my face into it. The raspberries-and-cream scent of my favorite shampoo cracks me like a porcelain doll.

Look at me, world: a bald ex-beauty queen kneeling on my bathroom floor with my head on the toilet seat, bawling into a bag of hair. This will not be in my autobiography.

"Oribella!" Mom rushes in the door. "Princess, what's happened?" Her voice is thick with worry.

"Nothing . . . everything," I gasp between sobs.

Mom kneels beside me. "Please, tell me what's wrong. Whatever it is, I promise I'll listen to every word."

"Things are okay. Really." It's hard to be convincing when I'm blubbering. "Ms. W c-called about the fit cap for my wig. And I was going to match the color to my hair. But when I looked in the bag and saw all the hair I lost . . ."

"It's all right, princess. Let it go. Cry it out," she croons. "My darling child. You've suffered so much. And I deserted you when you needed me. I will never forgive myself."

"I don't want to think about that anymore." I drag my sleeve across my wet cheeks. "Please just be my mom again."

"My poor, poor baby. I am and always will be." Mom rubs my back in long, slow circles like she did when I was little. Comforting, healing.

She pulls me onto her lap and cradles my head against her chest. "I love you, princess, now and into eternity. Living like this—like strangers—is tearing my heart out."

Deep in my core, the lump of anger that has been poisoning me shatters and melts away. "I missed you so much, Mom, I thought I would die."

"I missed you, too, princess. So, so much." She kisses the top of my head, and my heart knows she kissed me this way when I was a baby. "Please forgive me."

"I'm sorry, Mom. I said awful things I didn't mean."

She puts her fingers to my lips. "Hush. There's nothing to be sorry for."

I slip my arms around her. "I love you, Mom."

"I love you a thousand times more."

Our faces press together, and our tears combine like two streams flowing into the same deep river.

By the time the doorbell rings, we've stopped crying. We help each other to our feet. With our arms around each other's waists, we totter downstairs. Mom's a mess of mascara streaks, and loose pieces of hair are stuck to my face. But the empty void in my heart is full again.

When we open the door, Ms. W's eyes widen, and she backs off a step. Then she rushes forward and pulls Mom and me into a hug. "Just as I told you, Oribella. I'm so happy for you both."

43

$\mathcal{F}$ive weeks have passed since Mom and I started getting to know each other again. The family counselor we're seeing says building a new relationship won't be easy. Mom needs to learn to be a mother, and I have to figure out what being a teenager is about. But we're making progress.

One thing's certain: we're not Team Bettencourt anymore. So when I return to my career, Ms. W will be my agent and manager. And Mom will watch from the sidelines—when she's not busy living her own life.

Mom is doing so well at her new job that she's already gotten a raise. And she's been spending a lot of time with Sam, the guy who repairs their copy machine. Last week she asked if I'd mind if she stopped wearing her wedding ring. I was surprised how hard it was to tell her it was okay. Daddy will always be in our hearts, but it's time to let him go.

My life is busy, too. Phil has found time for me after all. So have Serena, Destiny, Shy, and Mari. In fact, this weekend we're having our third sleepover—at my house.

My wig is supposed to arrive next week. Strange, I can't imagine myself with hair now. So I've decided not to wear my wig to school until next fall. Everyone's used to seeing me bald, and I don't want to be stared at the last week of my sophomore year. Maybe over the summer I'll adjust to having hair again. Part of the time anyway.

Speaking of letting go, I sent my bag of hair to Locks of Love. Even though it's too much of a jumbled mess to be made into a wig, they can still sell it to help other people.

Ms. W talked me into doing the spokesmodel thing. She says it will do me good to share my story with girls and guys like me who are trying to cope with alopecia. And it will keep my modeling skills sharp for the catalog shoots I'll be doing for Zonkers in July and August—wearing my gorgeous new blond shoulder-length wig. I guess Bev was wrong when she said bald models couldn't get work.

Speaking of summer vacation, Ms. Summers arranged a scholarship for me to attend a three-week dance camp in New Hampshire at the end of June. But before I go I have to get used to dancing with a group again.

That's why this afternoon I'm taking my first group

lesson in six months. My heart pounds as I dump my bag beside the wall. Like me, some students are still arriving. Others are warming up—stripping off their street clothes, stretching, grabbing a drink of water. Ms. Summers' studio rings with their easy chatter.

Gypsy sees me first. Then one by one they all do. The chatter trickles away and dies. Most of the girls don't go to Highland, so they haven't seen me since . . . and although I've gotten used to strangers staring, I cringe.

"Hi, Ori." Gypsy isn't overflowing with enthusiasm, but she breaks the silence. For that, I'd almost hug her.

Ms. Summers bustles in, clapping her hands for attention. "Places, places, girls. We'll begin with 'Mid-City Rock.'"

The dancers scurry to their floor positions, leaving me standing alone by the wall. Ms. Summers is preparing to cue up the music when she finally notices me. "Oribella! So wonderful that you're here. Girls, you remember Oribella."

I'm greeted with a few ragged "hellos," but Ms. Summers is on to other things. "Oribella, you know the routines. Why don't you stand in the front beside Gypsy? Just like old times."

Just like old times.

Nothing about me is just like old times. "Ms. Summers, if it's okay, I'd prefer to stand in the back."

Ms. Summers shrugs her shoulders. "Certainly. If that's what you'd prefer."

As I walk to the back, Gypsy steps out of line. "I'll move, too, Ms. Summers. Since Ori and I are about the same height." She takes her position beside me. "I've been practicing," she whispers. "You'll see."

"Fine! Fine!" Ms. Summers waves her arms. "Now, is everyone where they want to be?"

A smile lights me from the inside out. I'm exactly where I want to be.

Printed in the United States
By Bookmasters